D1505174

THE
METAMORPHOSIS

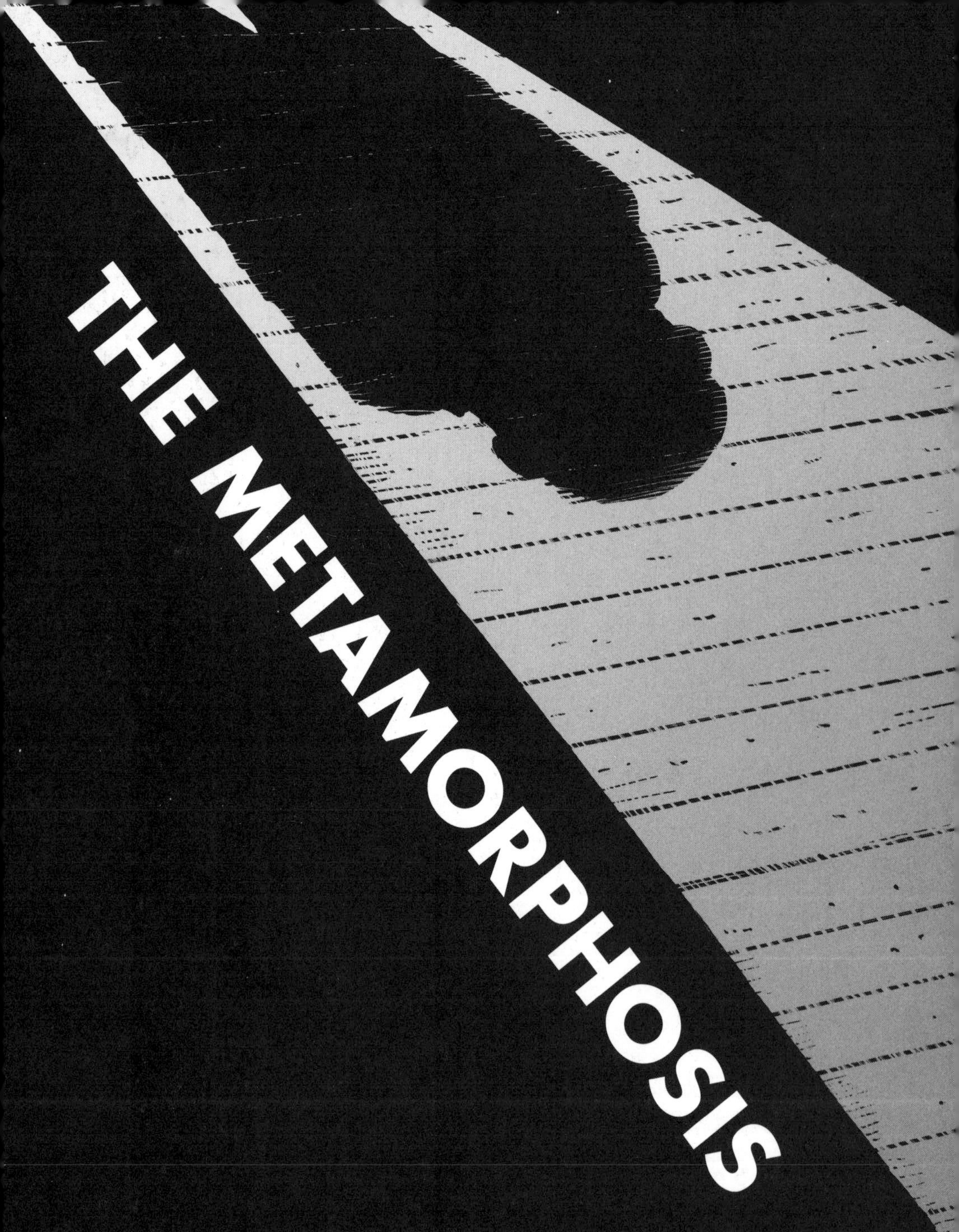

THE METAMORPHOSIS

FRANZ KAFKA

ADAPTED BY **PETER KUPER**

CROWN

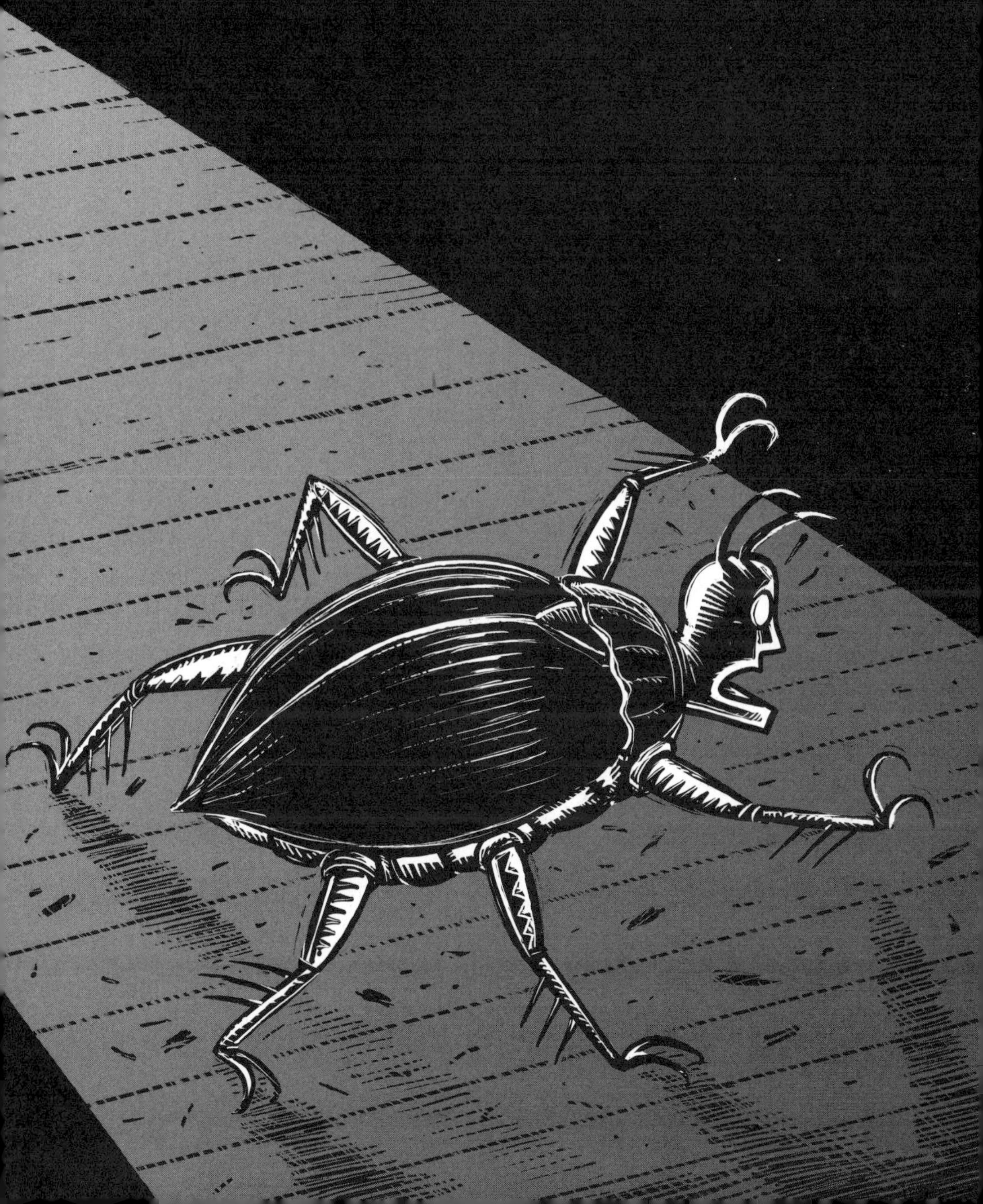

Dedicated to Gregor Samsas everywhere

 Published by Crown Publishers, New York, New York. Member of the Crown Publishing Group, a division of Random House, Inc. www.randomhouse.com. CROWN is a trademark and the Crown colophon is a registered trademark of Random House, Inc. Printed in the United States of America. Library of Congress Cataloging-in-Publication Data is available upon request.
ISBN 1-4000-4795-1
10 9 8 7 6 5 4 3 2 1
First Edition

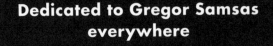

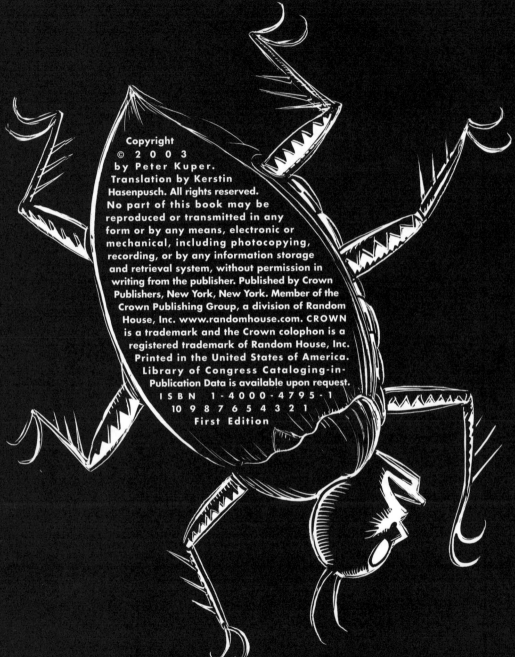

THE INTRODUCTION

In 1904, more than a decade before Franz Kafka published *The Metamorphosis* in Prague, across the ocean a cartoonist named Winsor McCay created "Dream of the Rarebit Fiend," a comic strip that appeared in New York's *Evening Telegram.* In each one-page installment a character was trapped in a world that grew more surreal with each panel—a gentleman's leg inflates and demolishes a mansion, a suitor's lover crumbles into confetti and blows away, a lady's alligator handbag morphs into a monster and devours her. Finally, in the last panel, the character awakens to reality, vowing never again to eat the nightmare-inducing rarebit cheese before bedtime.

Of course, Franz Kafka never allowed his characters to enjoy the relief of awakening to normalcy from their disturbing dreams. Still, the two artists had much in common, including a shared genius for rendering the anxious intersection of reality and dreamscape. Kafka may never have been a comic strip fan, but his angst-ridden characters in reality-bending scenarios are ideally suited to this medium. This adaptation of *The Metamorphosis* couldn't exist without Kafka's illuminating words, but owes a visual debt to McCay's trailblazing excursions into the absurd darkness of slumberland. I have drawn tremendous inspiration from both these pioneers, fascinated by their ability to address our human condition with unexpected twists, brilliant artistry, and deadpan humor.

Nearly a century later, the works of Kafka and McCay seem as fresh as if they were created to reflect our current zeitgeist. Kafka's tales of nightmare trials and monolithic bureaucracies feel no more surreal than headlines from our daily newspapers. It makes one wish that simply avoiding rarebit cheese were the remedy.

—Peter Kuper

When Gregor Samsa
awoke one morning from
disturbing dreams,
he found himself
transformed . . .

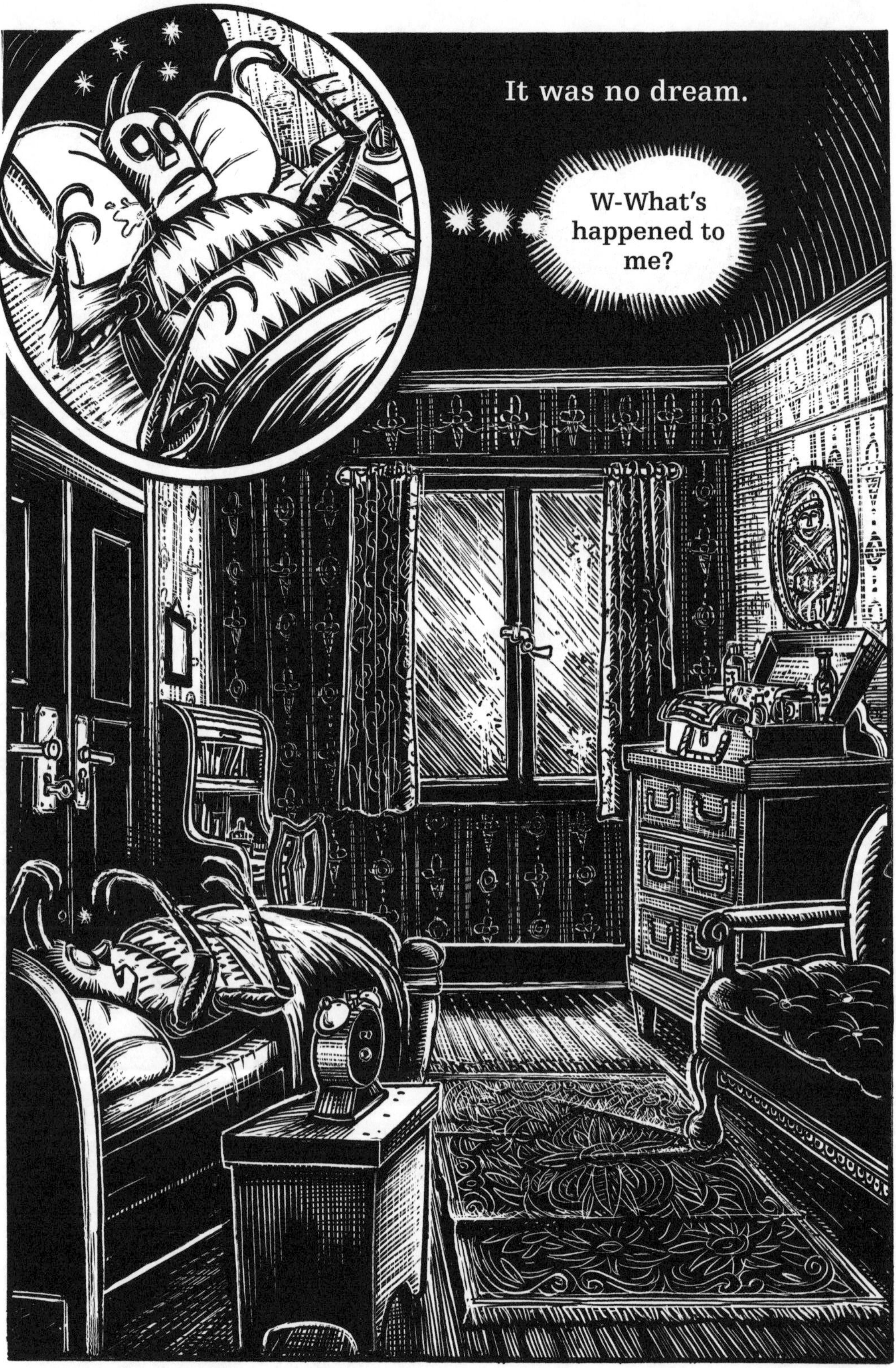
It was no dream.
W-What's happened to me?

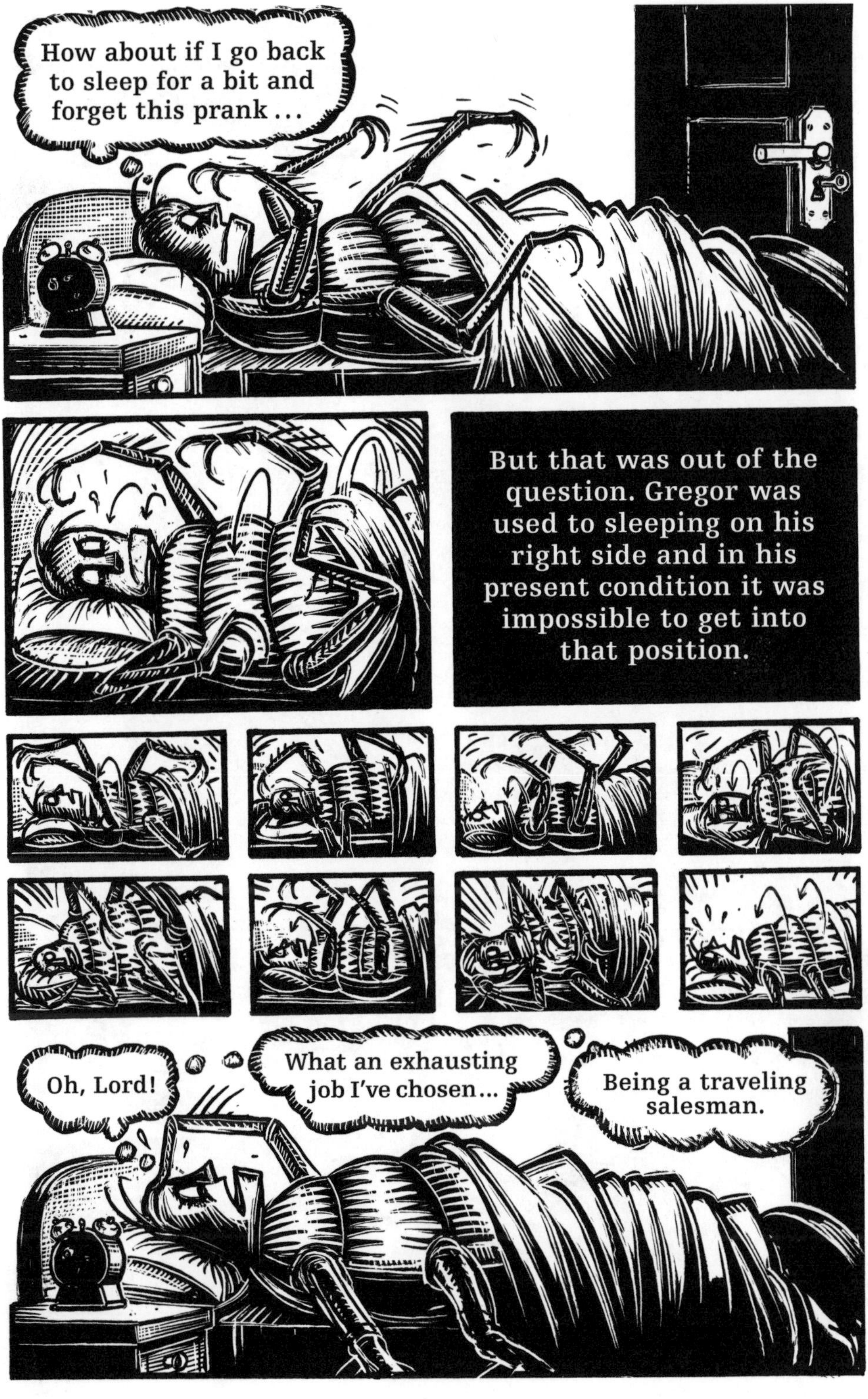
How about if I go back to sleep for a bit and forget this prank . . .
But that was out of the question. Gregor was used to sleeping on his right side and in his present condition it was impossible to get into that position.
Oh, Lord!
What an exhausting job I've chosen...
Being a traveling salesman.

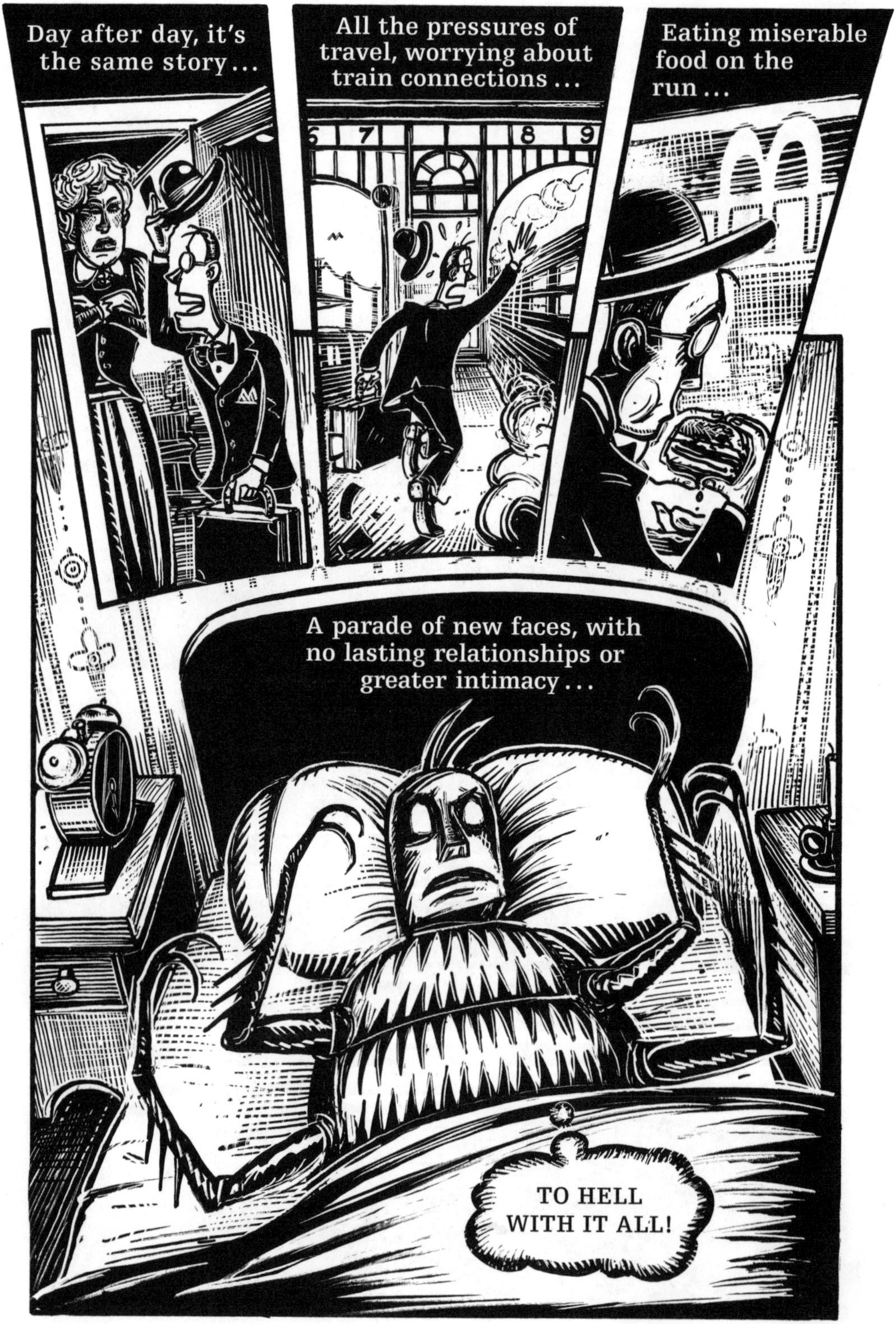
Day after day, it's the same story...
All the pressures of travel, worrying about train connections...
Eating miserable food on the run...
A parade of new faces, with no lasting relationships or greater intimacy...
TO HELL WITH IT ALL!

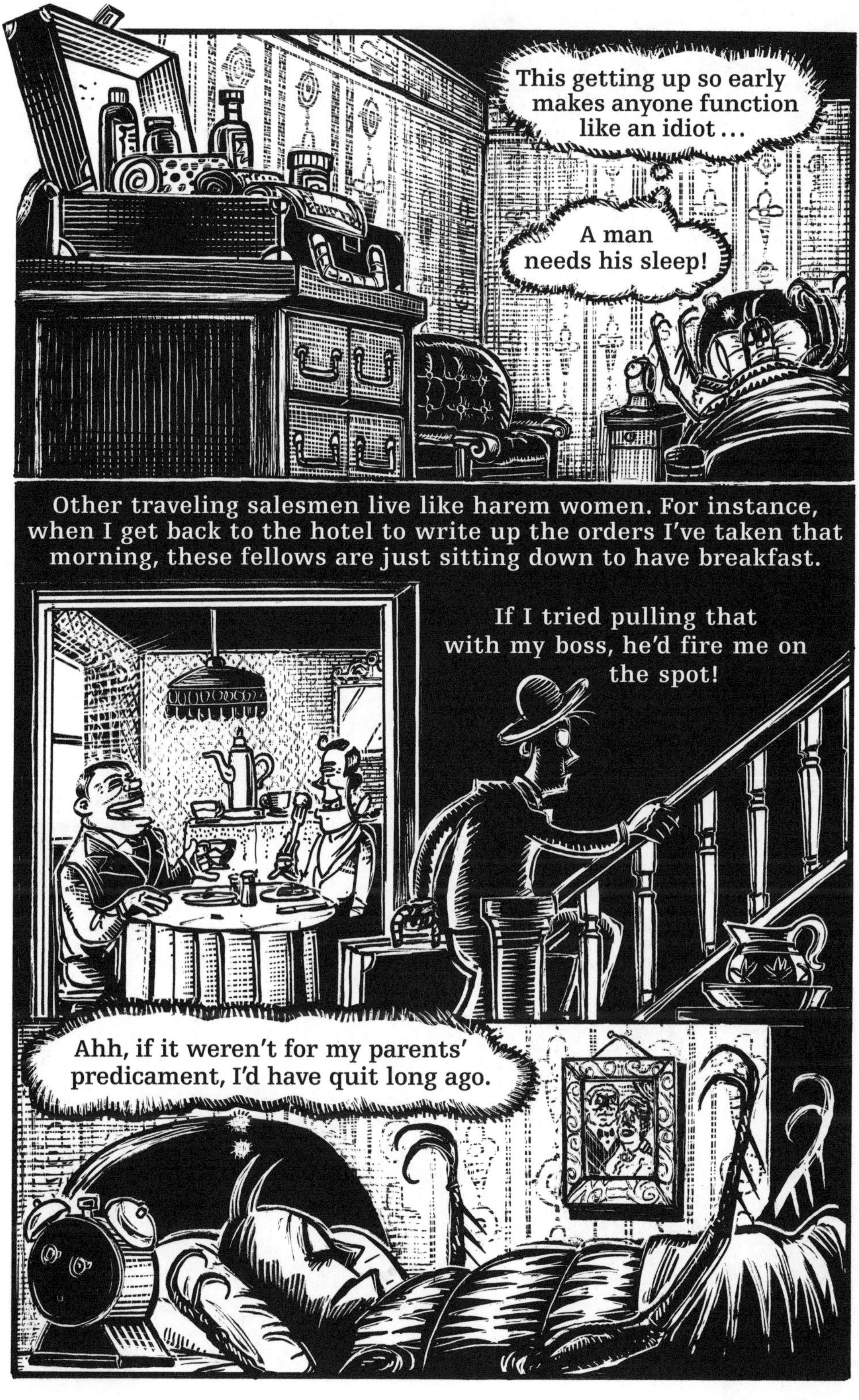

This getting up so early makes anyone function like an idiot . . .
A man needs his sleep!
Other traveling salesmen live like harem women. For instance, when I get back to the hotel to write up the orders I've taken that morning, these fellows are just sitting down to have breakfast.
If I tried pulling that with my boss, he'd fire me on the spot!
Ahh, if it weren't for my parents' predicament, I'd have quit long ago.

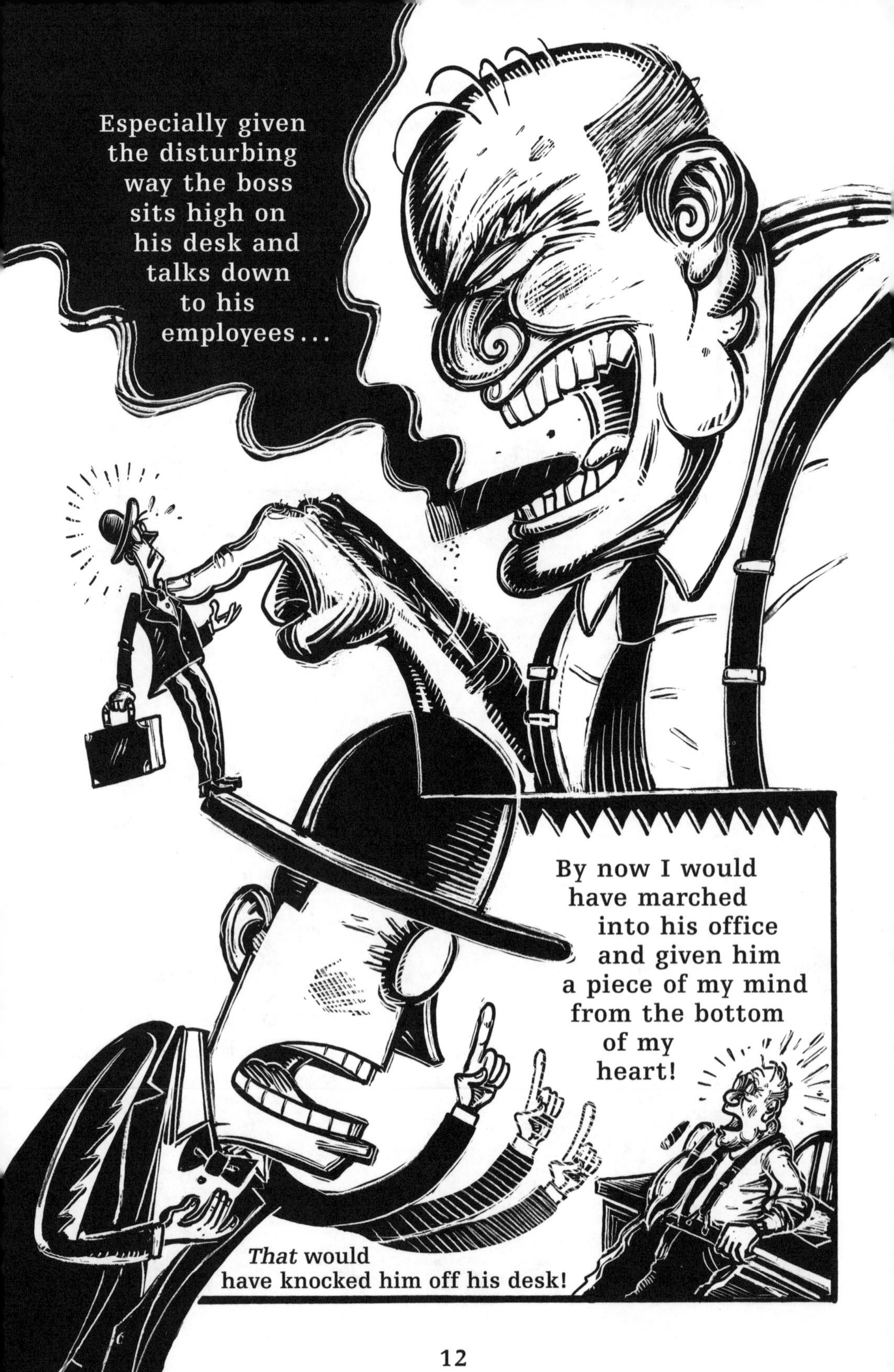
Especially given the disturbing way the boss sits high on his desk and talks down to his employees...
By now I would have marched into his office and given him a piece of my mind from the bottom of my heart!
That would have knocked him off his desk!

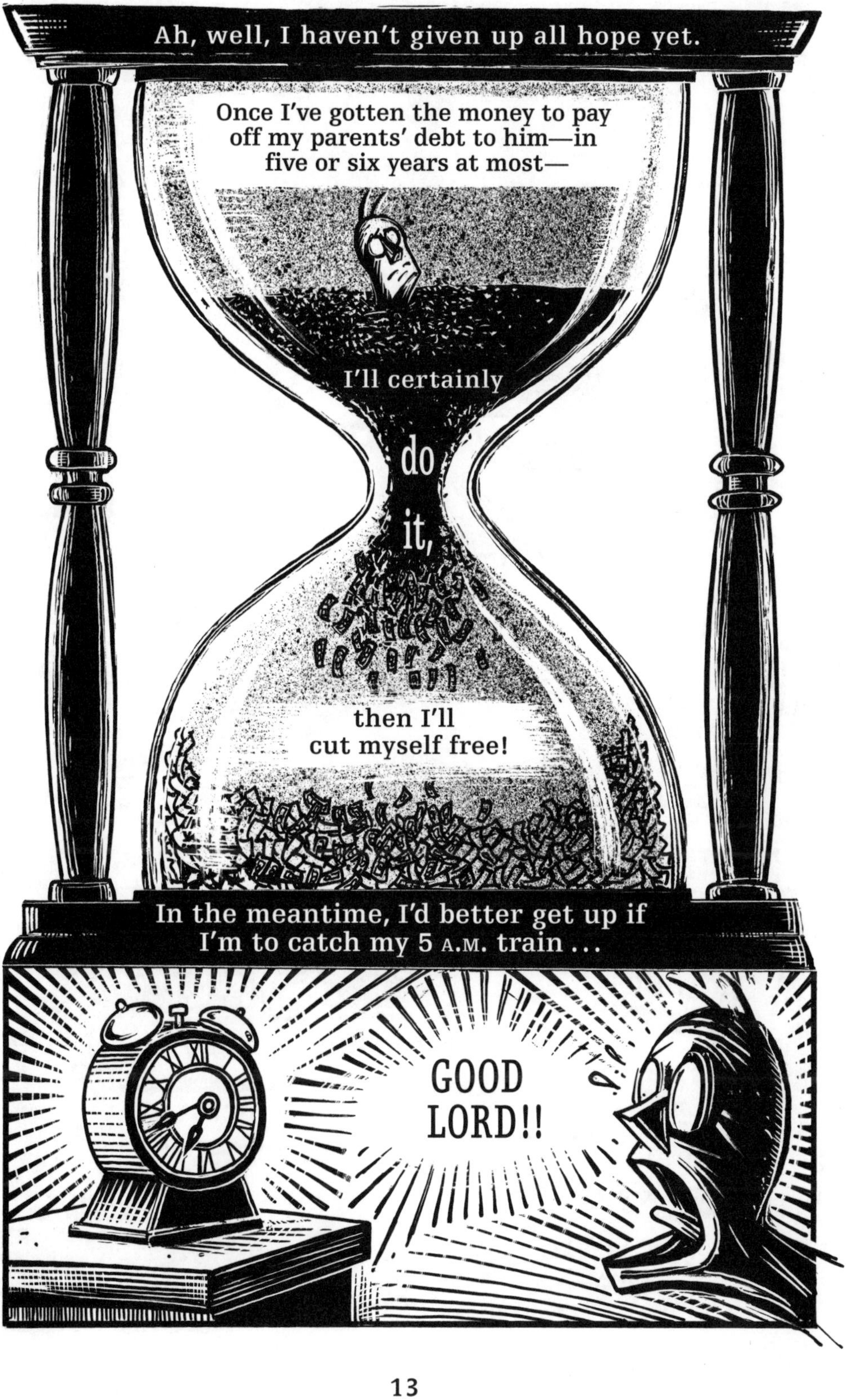

Ah, well, I haven't given up all hope yet.
Once I've gotten the money to pay off my parents' debt to him—in five or six years at most—
I'll certainly
do
it,
then I'll cut myself free!
In the meantime, I'd better get up if I'm to catch my 5 A.M. train . . .
GOOD LORD!!

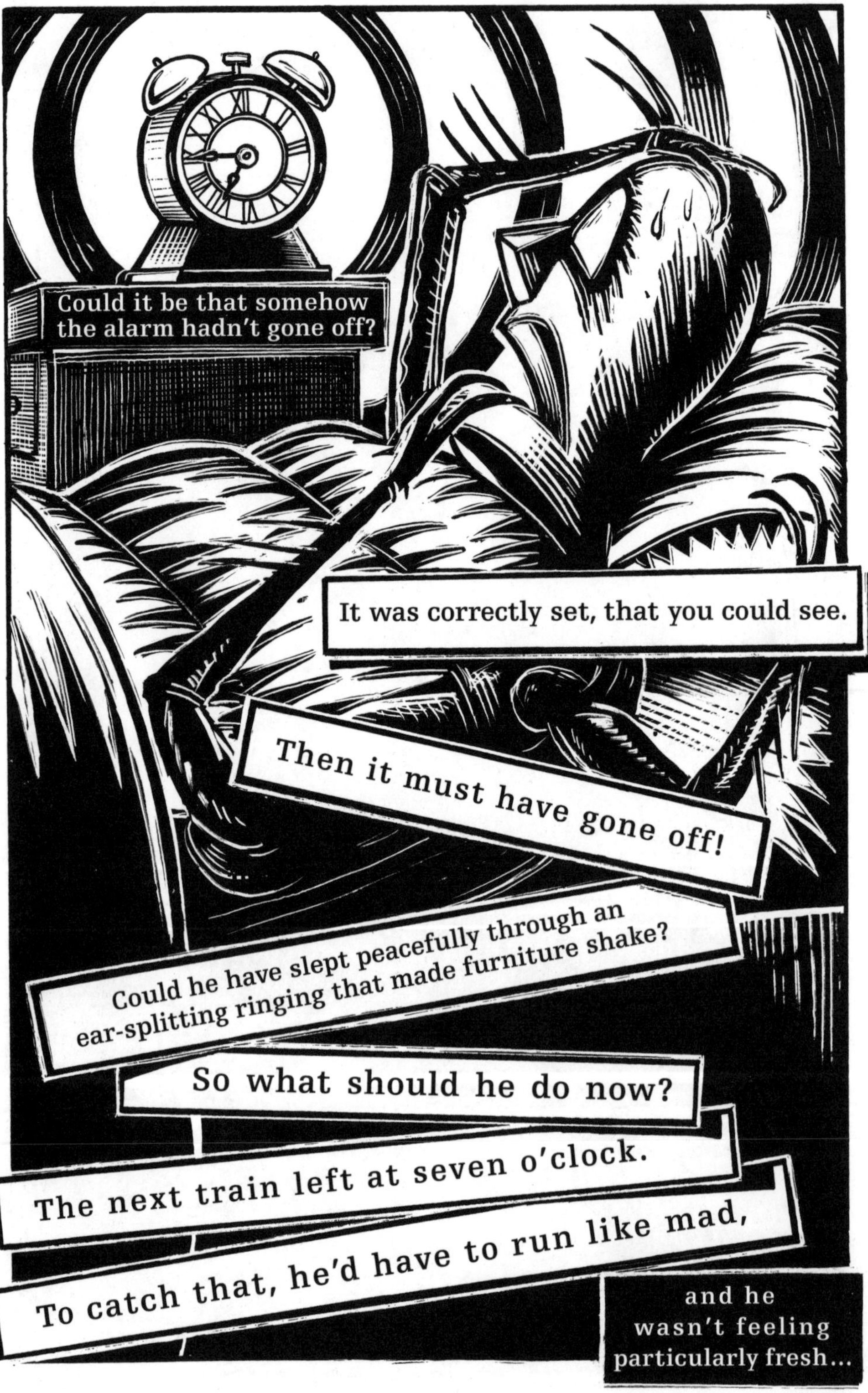

Could it be that somehow the alarm hadn't gone off?
It was correctly set, that you could see.
Then it must have gone off!
Could he have slept peacefully through an ear-splitting ringing that made furniture shake?
So what should he do now?
The next train left at seven o'clock.
To catch that, he'd have to run like mad,
and he wasn't feeling particularly fresh...

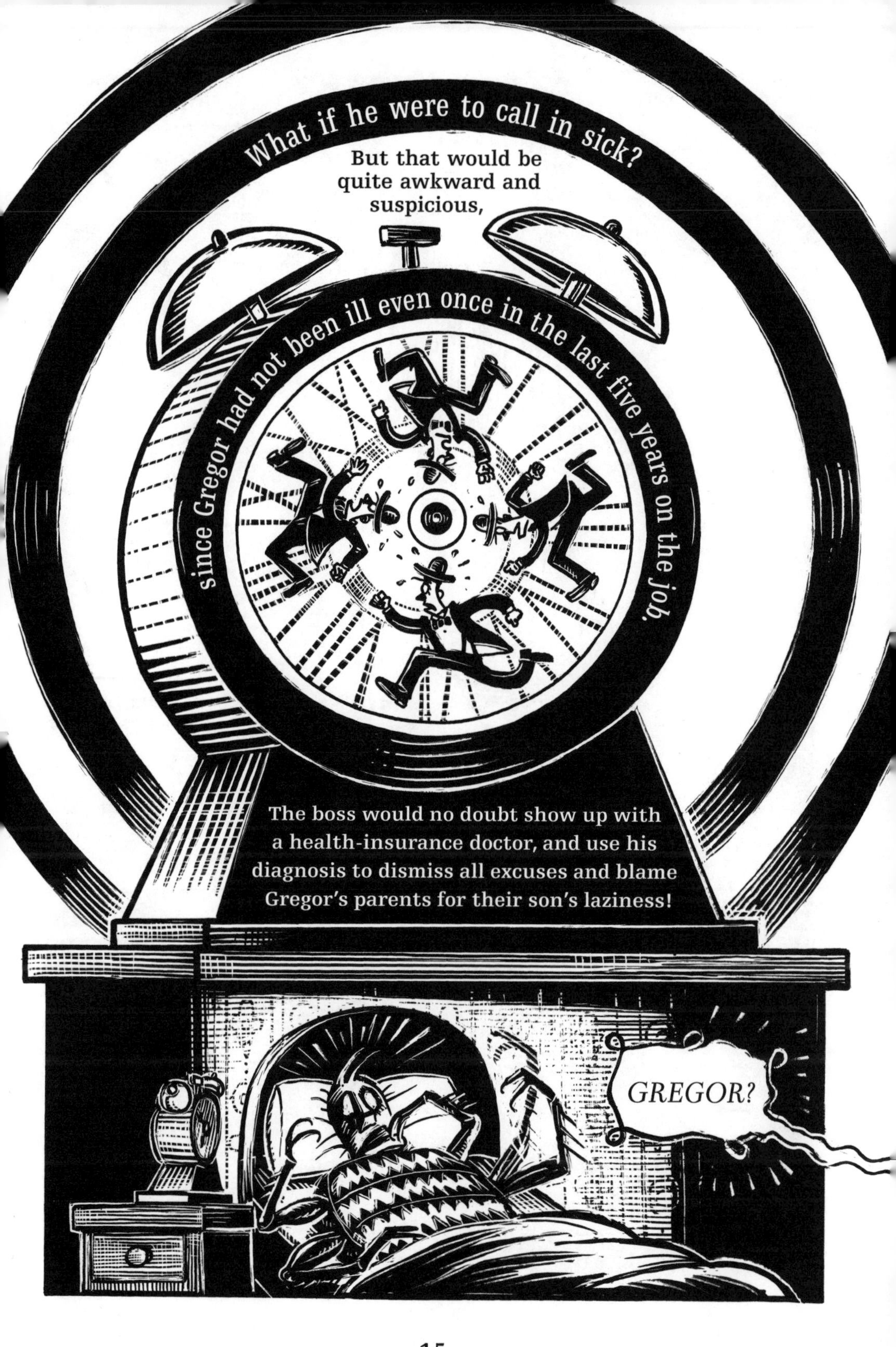

What if he were to call in sick?
But that would be quite awkward and suspicious,
since Gregor had not been ill even once in the last five years on the job.
The boss would no doubt show up with a health-insurance doctor, and use his diagnosis to dismiss all excuses and blame Gregor's parents for their son's laziness!
GREGOR?

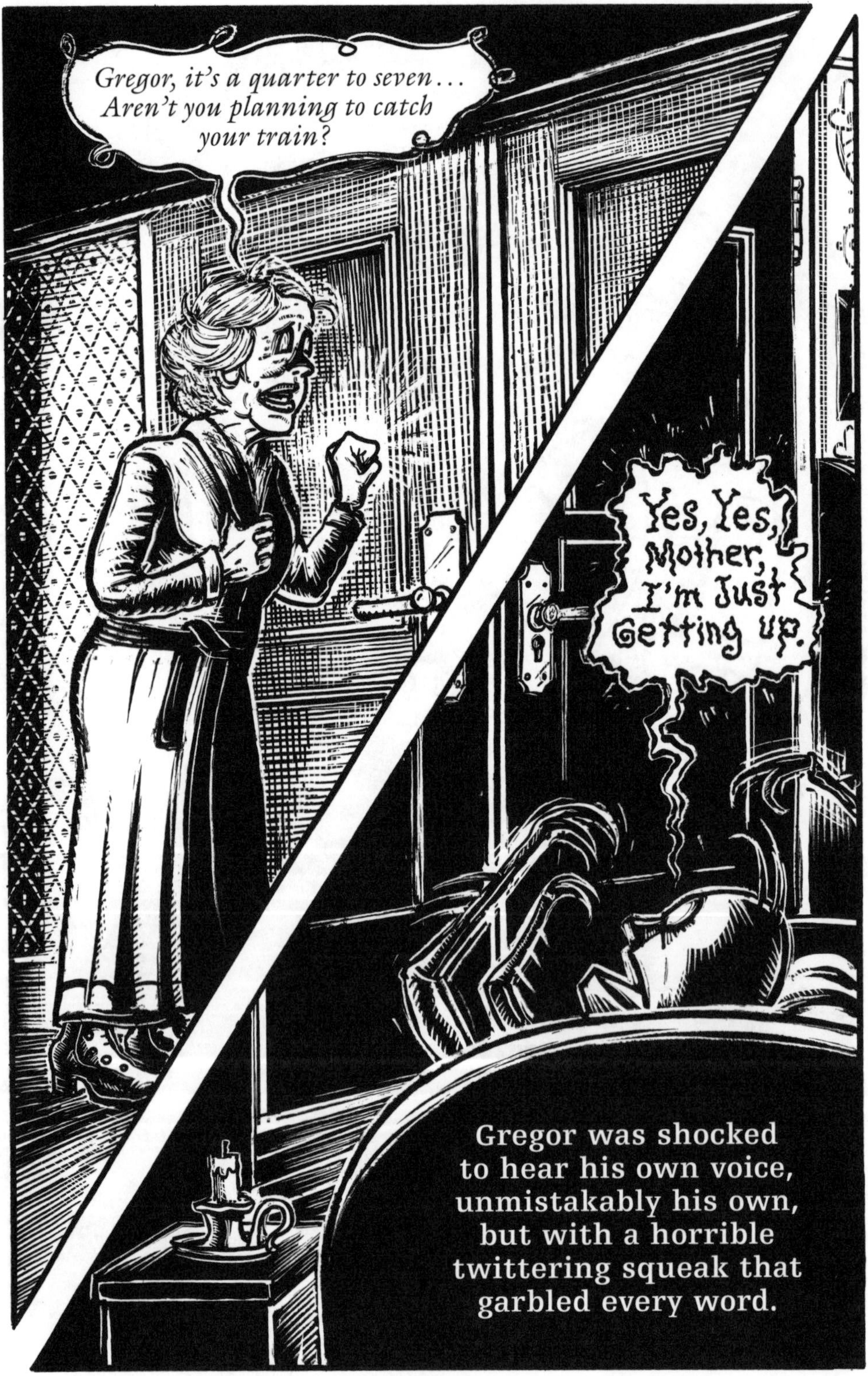
Gregor, it's a quarter to seven... Aren't you planning to catch your train?
Yes, Yes, Mother, I'm Just Getting up.
Gregor was shocked to hear his own voice, unmistakably his own, but with a horrible twittering squeak that garbled every word.

The change in Gregor's voice must have been muffled by the wooden door because his mother was reassured and shuffled off. However, their little exchange made his father and sister aware that Gregor had not, as they assumed, left for work.

GREGOR, GREGOR— what's going on?

GREGOR!

Gregor, it's Grete, are you alright?

Do you need *anything*?

Please, Gregor, open the door.

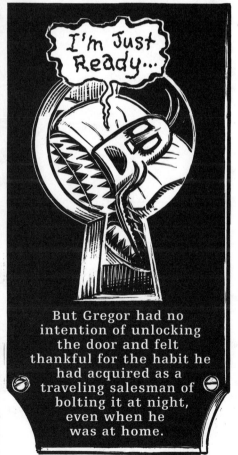

I'm Just Ready...

But Gregor had no intention of unlocking the door and felt thankful for the habit he had acquired as a traveling salesman of bolting it at night, even when he was at home.

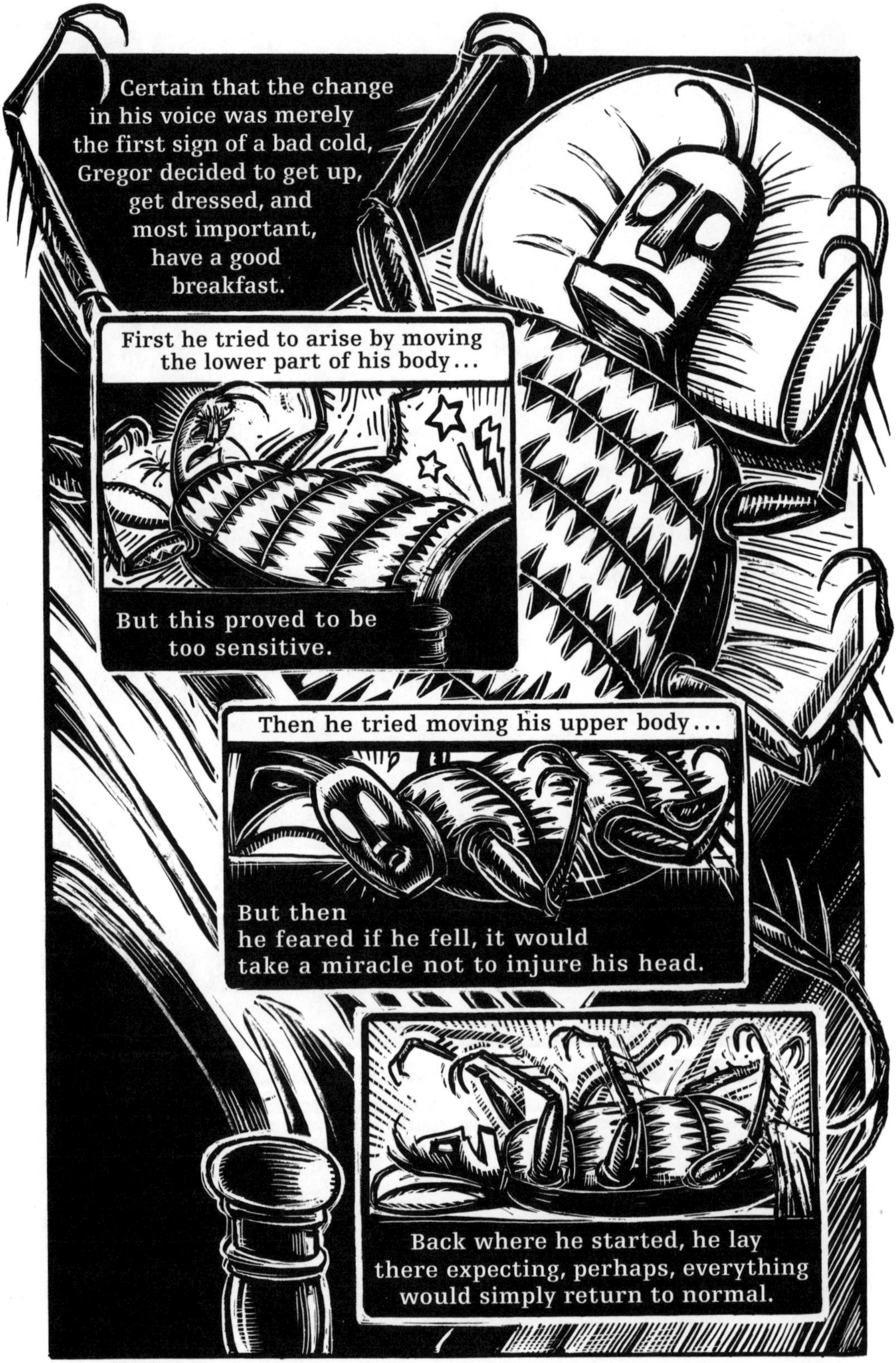
Certain that the change in his voice was merely the first sign of a bad cold, Gregor decided to get up, get dressed, and most important, have a good breakfast.
First he tried to arise by moving the lower part of his body...
But this proved to be too sensitive.
Then he tried moving his upper body...
But then he feared if he fell, it would take a miracle not to injure his head.
Back where he started, he lay there expecting, perhaps, everything would simply return to normal.

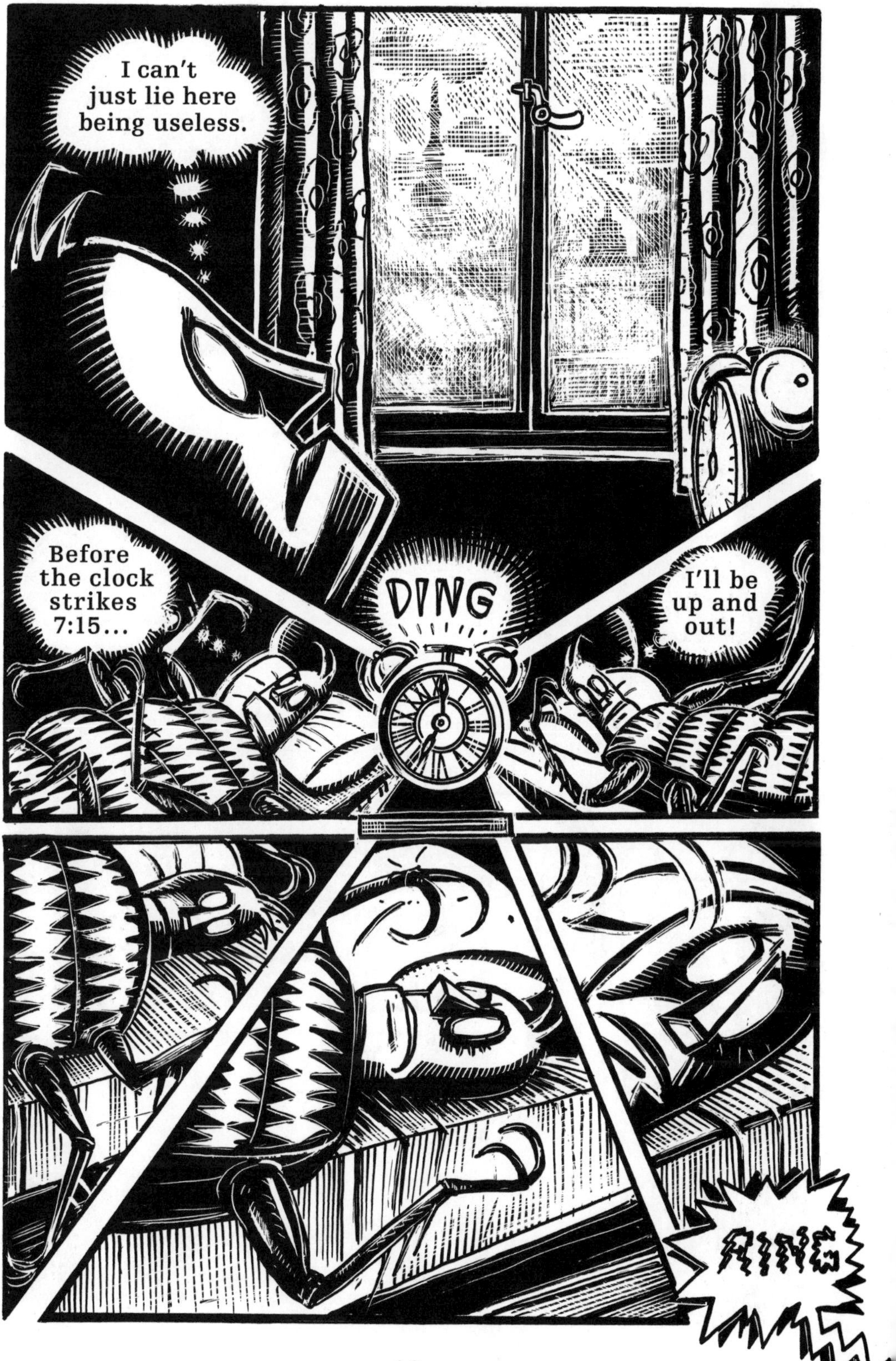
I can't just lie here being useless.
Before the clock strikes 7:15...
DING
I'll be up and out!
RING

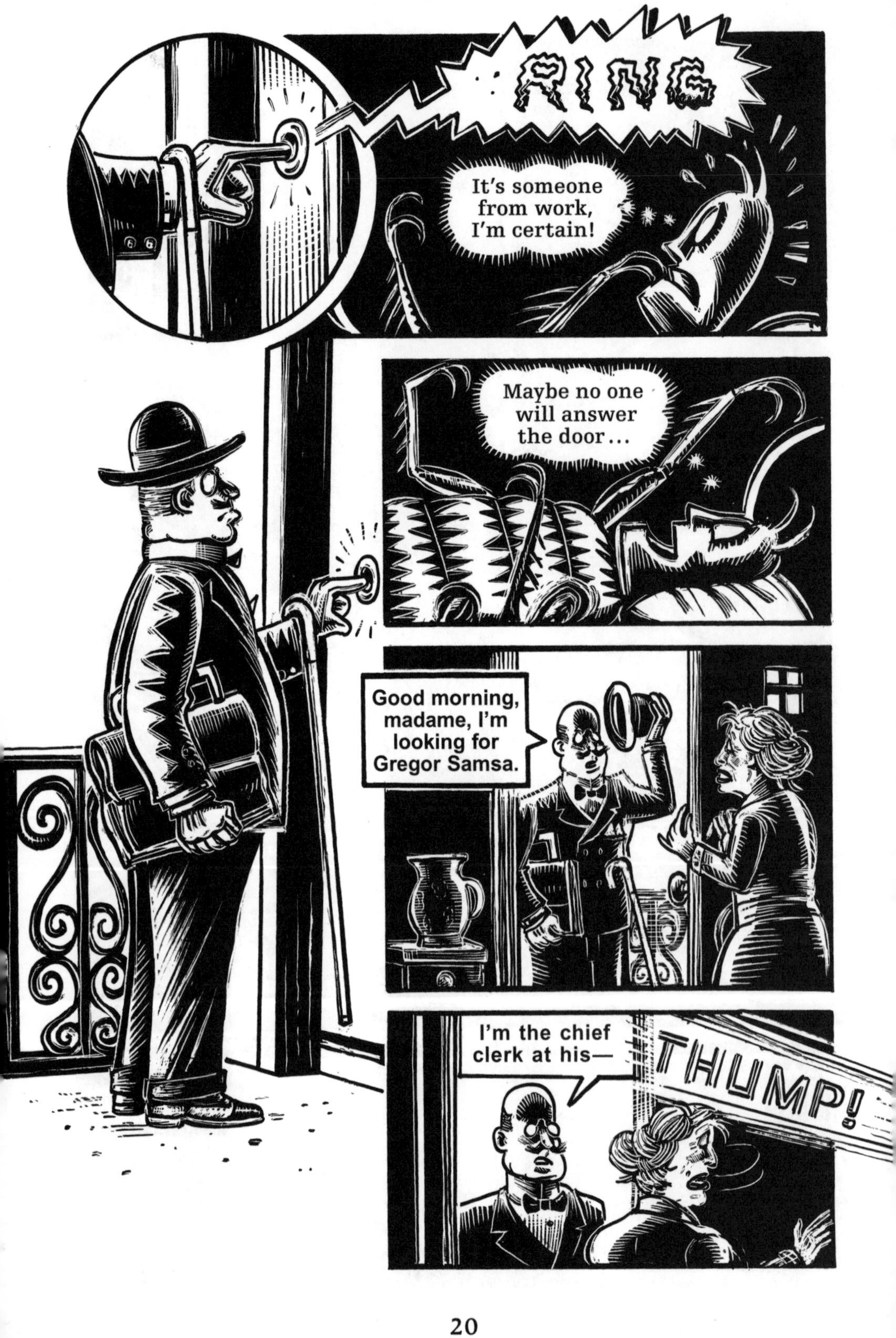
RING
It's someone from work, I'm certain!
Maybe no one will answer the door...
Good morning, madame, I'm looking for Gregor Samsa.
I'm the chief clerk at his—
THUMP!

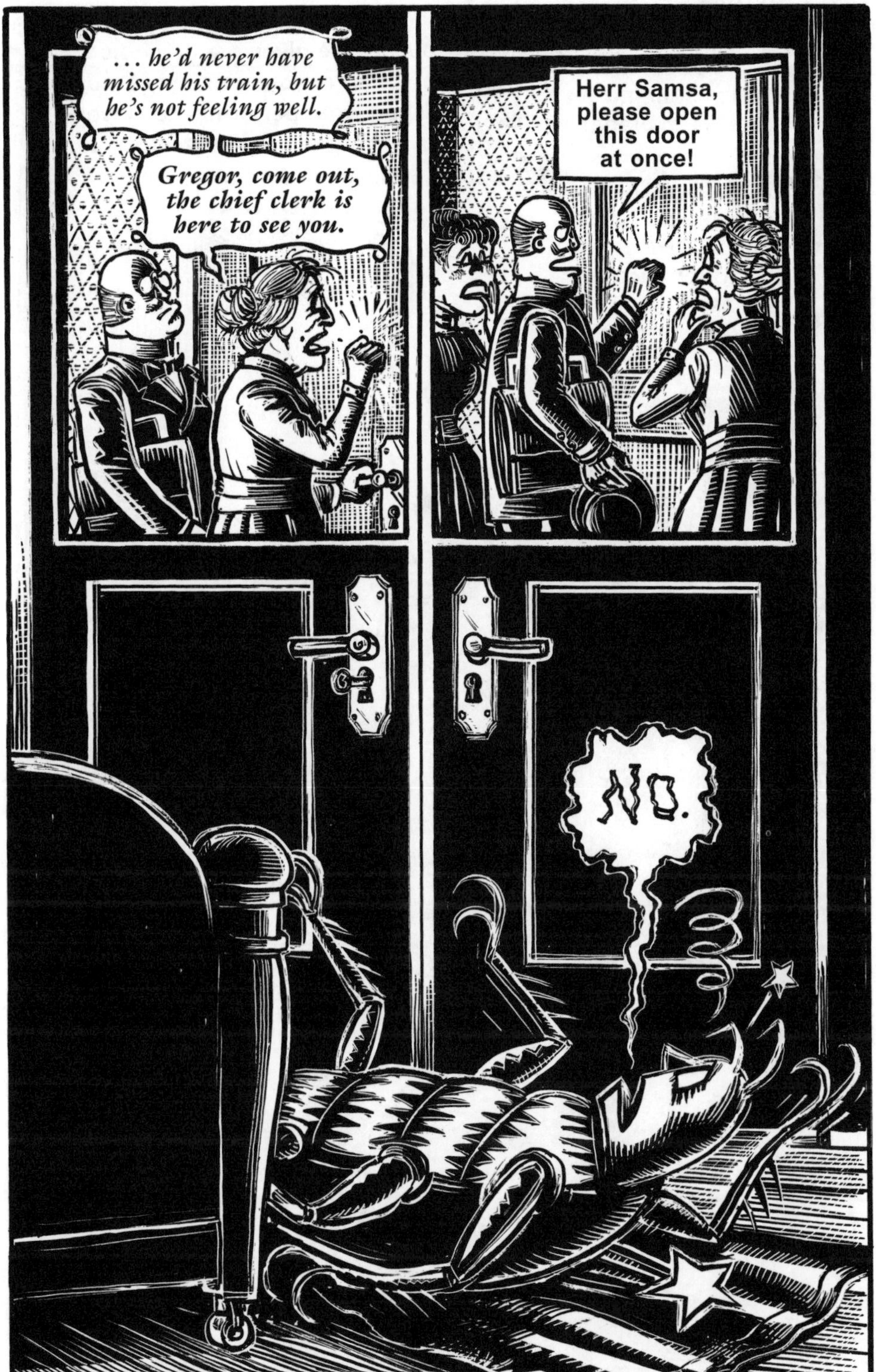
... he'd never have missed his train, but he's not feeling well.
Gregor, come out, the chief clerk is here to see you.
Herr Samsa, please open this door at once!
NO.

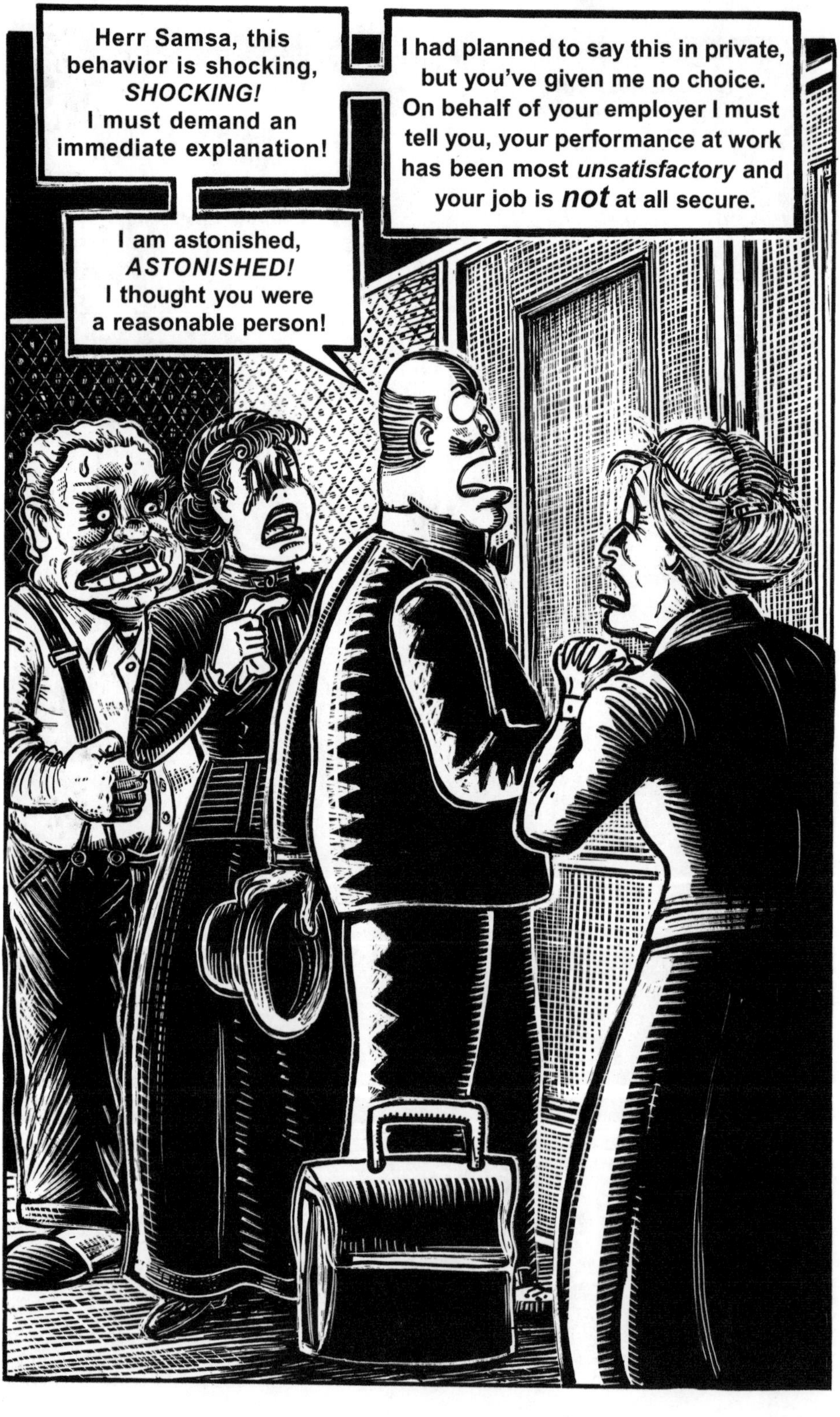
Herr Samsa, this behavior is shocking, SHOCKING! I must demand an immediate explanation!
I am astonished, ASTONISHED! I thought you were a reasonable person!
I had planned to say this in private, but you've given me no choice. On behalf of your employer I must tell you, your performance at work has been most unsatisfactory and your job is not at all secure.

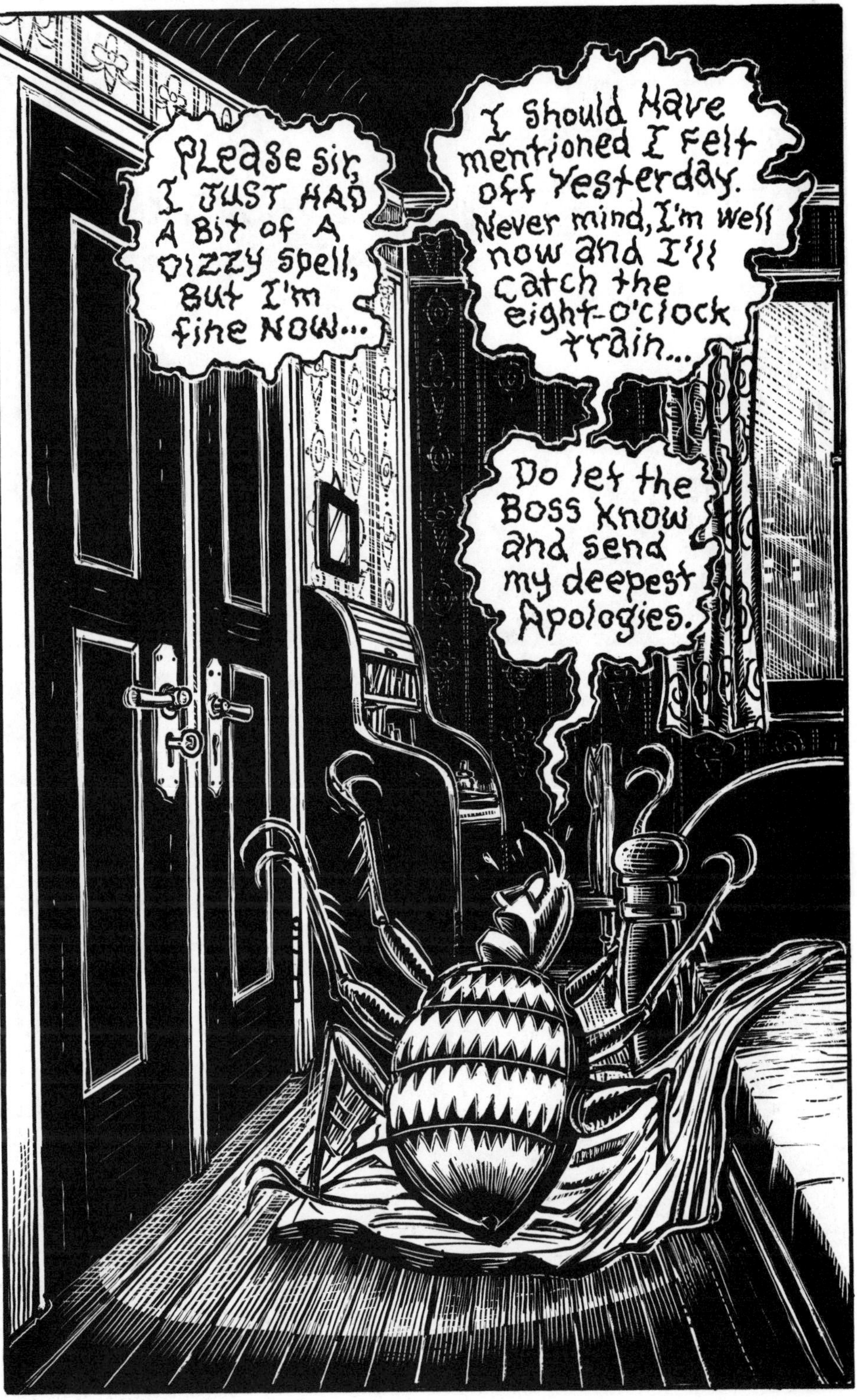
PLEASE SIR, I JUST HAD A BIT OF A DIZZY SPELL, BUT I'M FINE NOW...
I SHOULD HAVE MENTIONED I FELT OFF YESTERDAY. NEVER MIND, I'M WELL NOW AND I'LL CATCH THE EIGHT-O'CLOCK TRAIN...
DO LET THE BOSS KNOW AND SEND MY DEEPEST APOLOGIES.

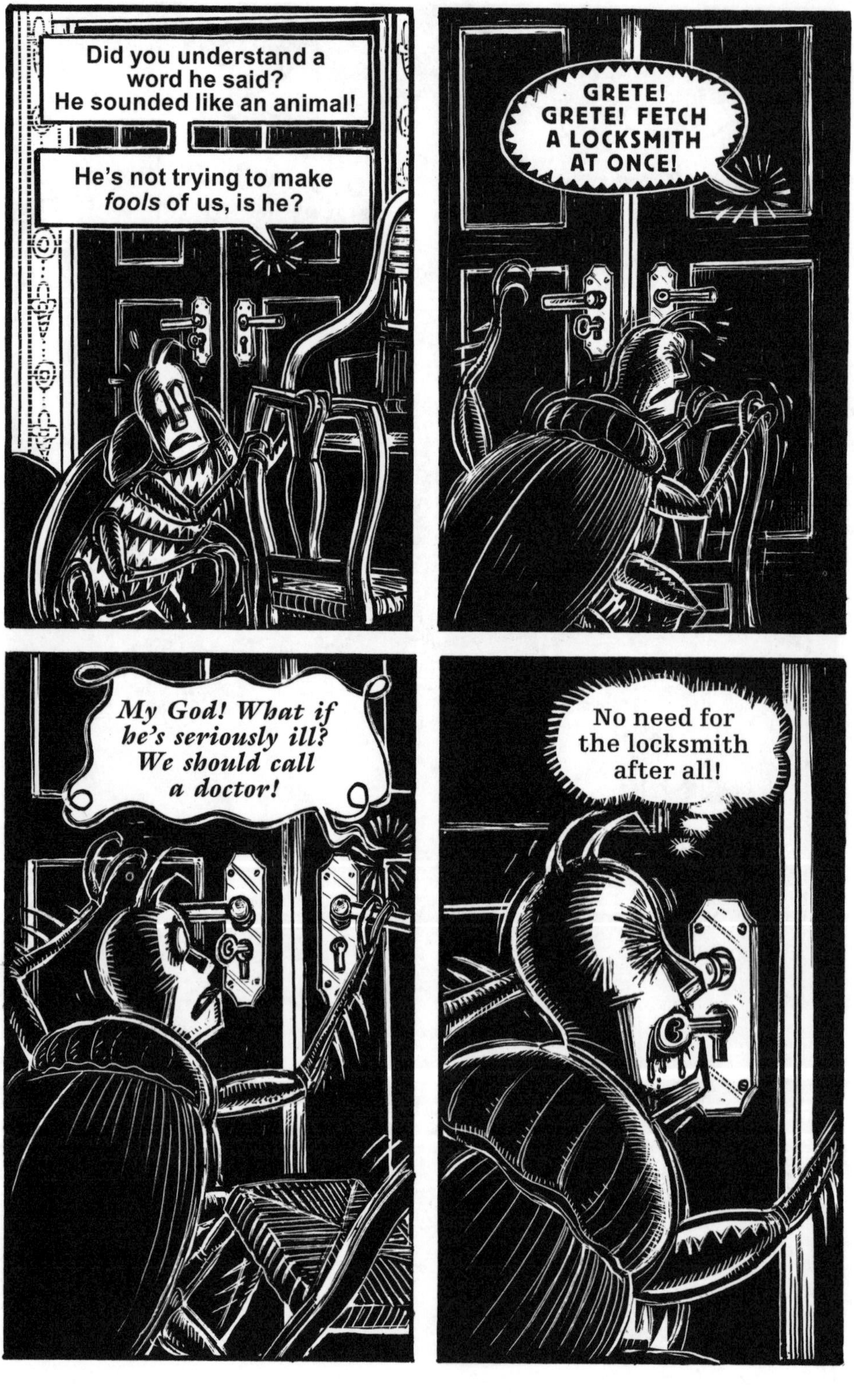
Did you understand a word he said? He sounded like an animal!
He's not trying to make *fools* of us, is he?
GRETE! GRETE! FETCH A LOCKSMITH AT ONCE!
My God! What if he's seriously ill? We should call a doctor!
No need for the locksmith after all!

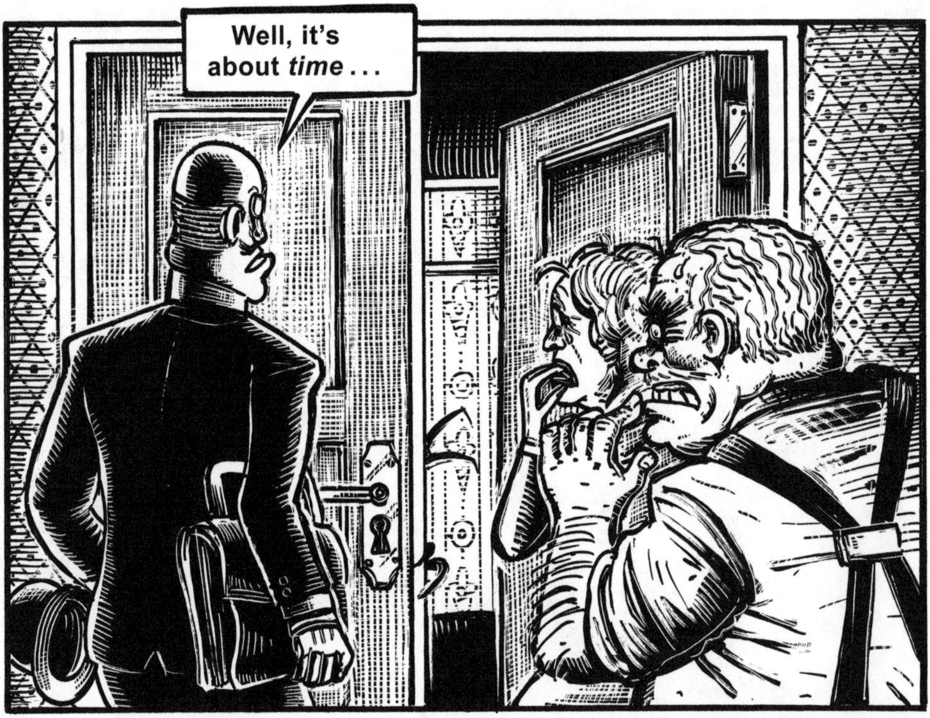
Well, it's about *time* . . .

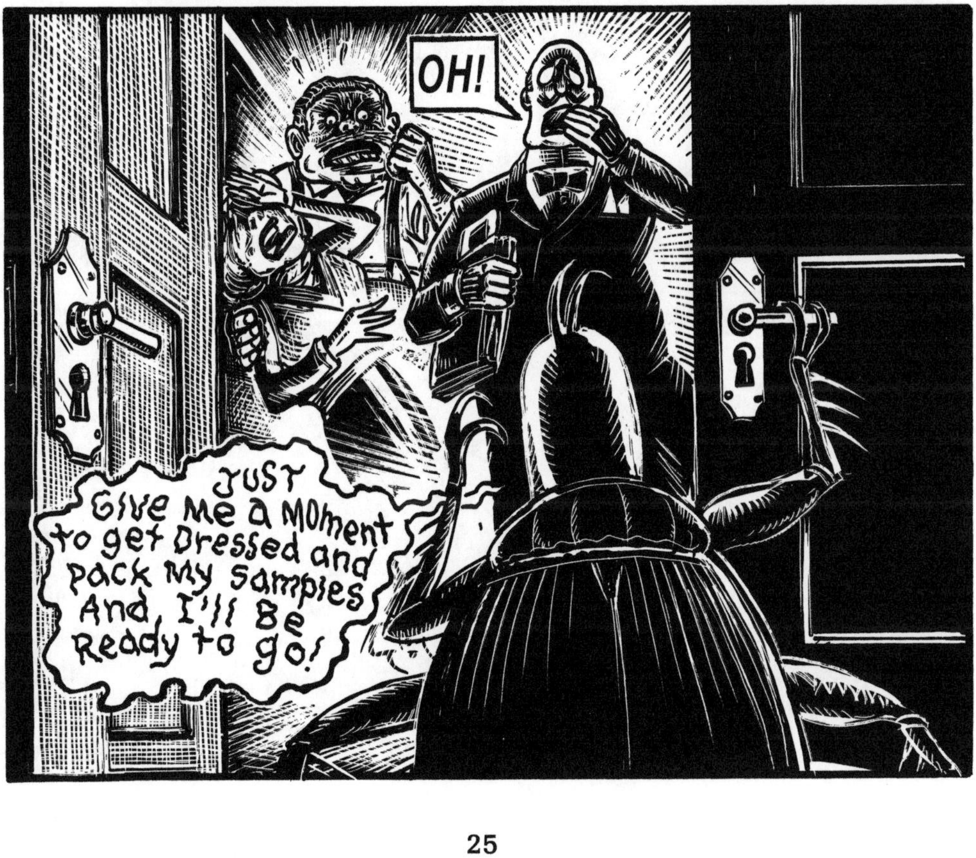
OH!
JUST GIVE ME A MOMENT TO GET DRESSED AND PACK MY SAMPLES AND, I'LL BE READY TO GO!

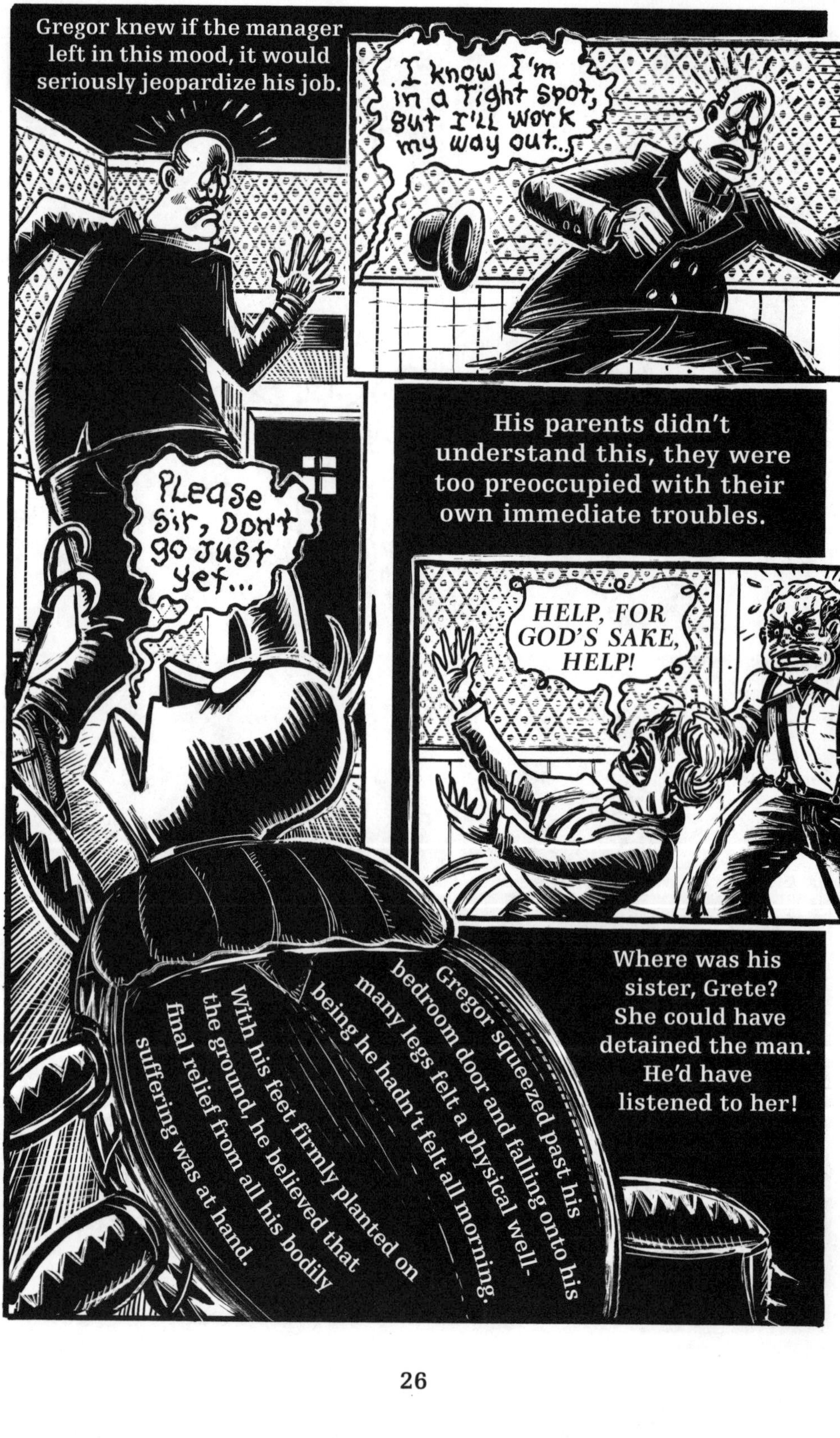
Gregor knew if the manager left in this mood, it would seriously jeopardize his job.
I know I'm in a Tight spot, but I'll work my way out...
Please sir, Don't go just yet...
His parents didn't understand this, they were too preoccupied with their own immediate troubles.
HELP, FOR GOD'S SAKE, HELP!
Where was his sister, Grete? She could have detained the man. He'd have listened to her!
Gregor squeezed past his bedroom door and falling onto his many legs felt a physical well-being he hadn't felt all morning.
With his feet firmly planted on the ground, he believed that final relief from all his bodily suffering was at hand.

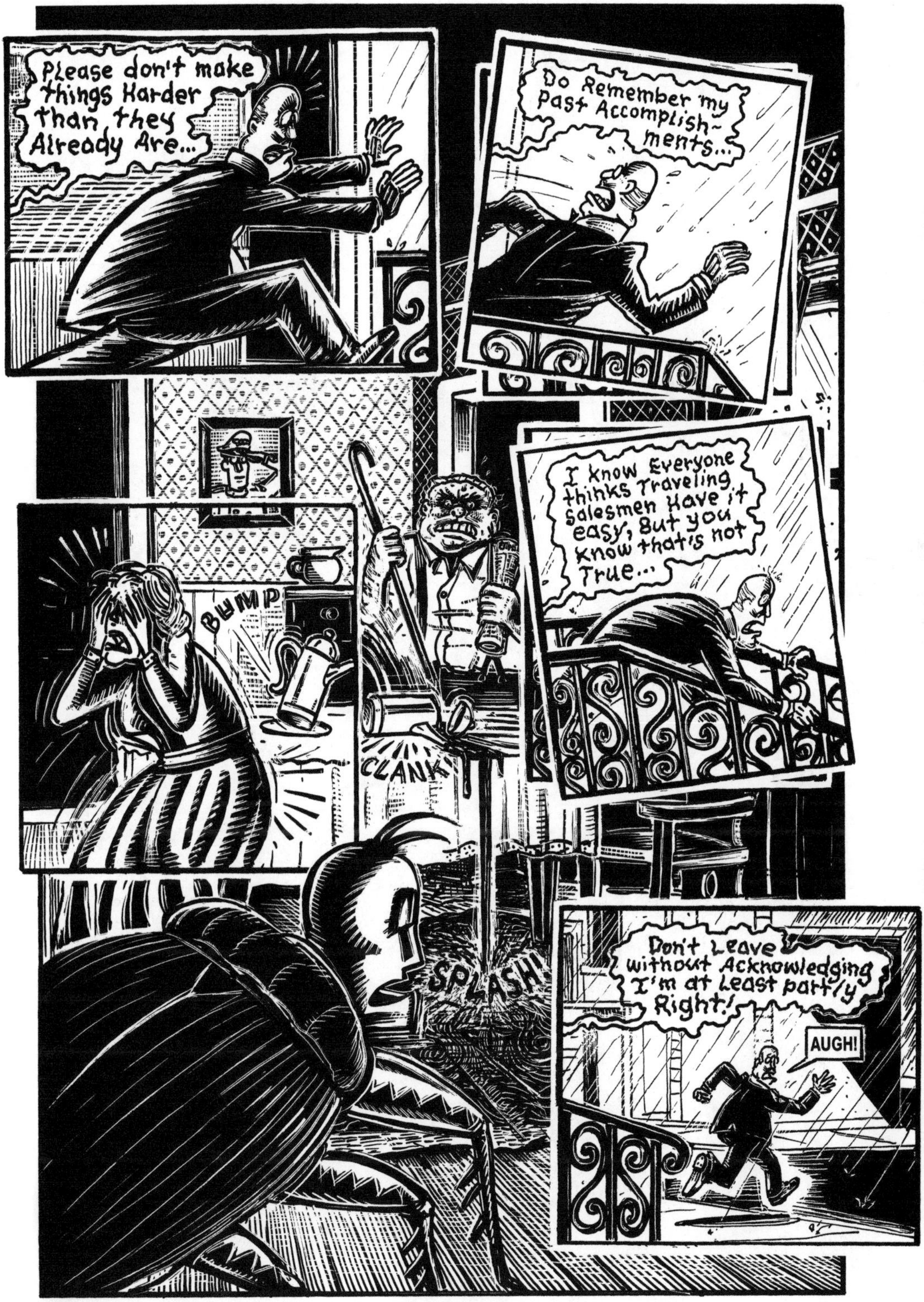
Please don't make things Harder than they Already Are...
Do Remember my Past Accomplish-ments...
I know Everyone thinks Traveling Salesmen Have it easy, But you know that's not True...
BUMP
CLANK
SPLASH!
Don't Leave without Acknowledging I'm at Least partly Right!
AUGH!

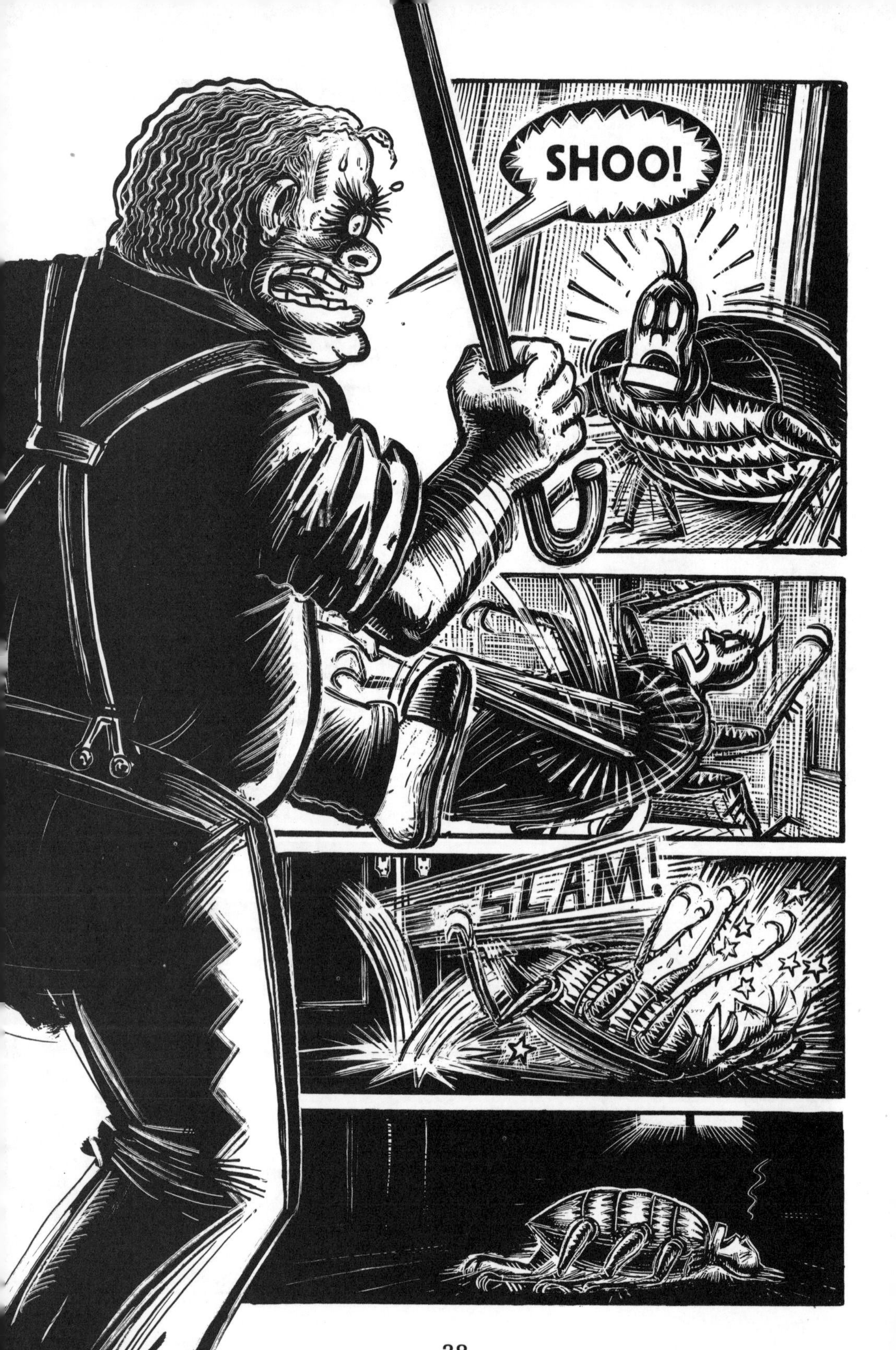
SHOO!
SLAM!

II

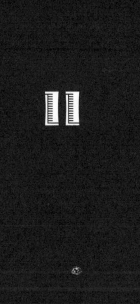

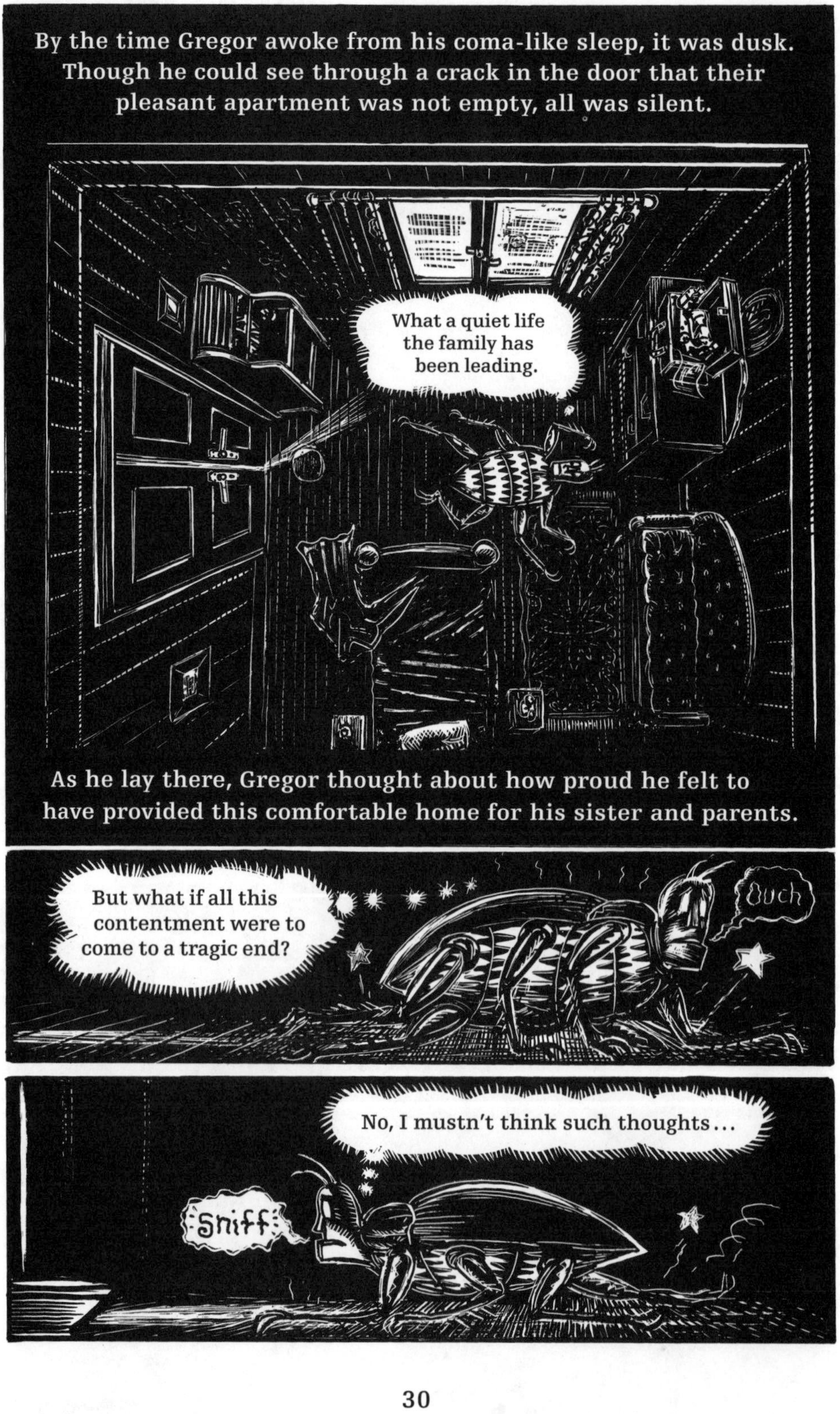

By the time Gregor awoke from his coma-like sleep, it was dusk. Though he could see through a crack in the door that their pleasant apartment was not empty, all was silent.
What a quiet life the family has been leading.
As he lay there, Gregor thought about how proud he felt to have provided this comfortable home for his sister and parents.
But what if all this contentment were to come to a tragic end?
Ouch
No, I mustn't think such thoughts...
Sniff

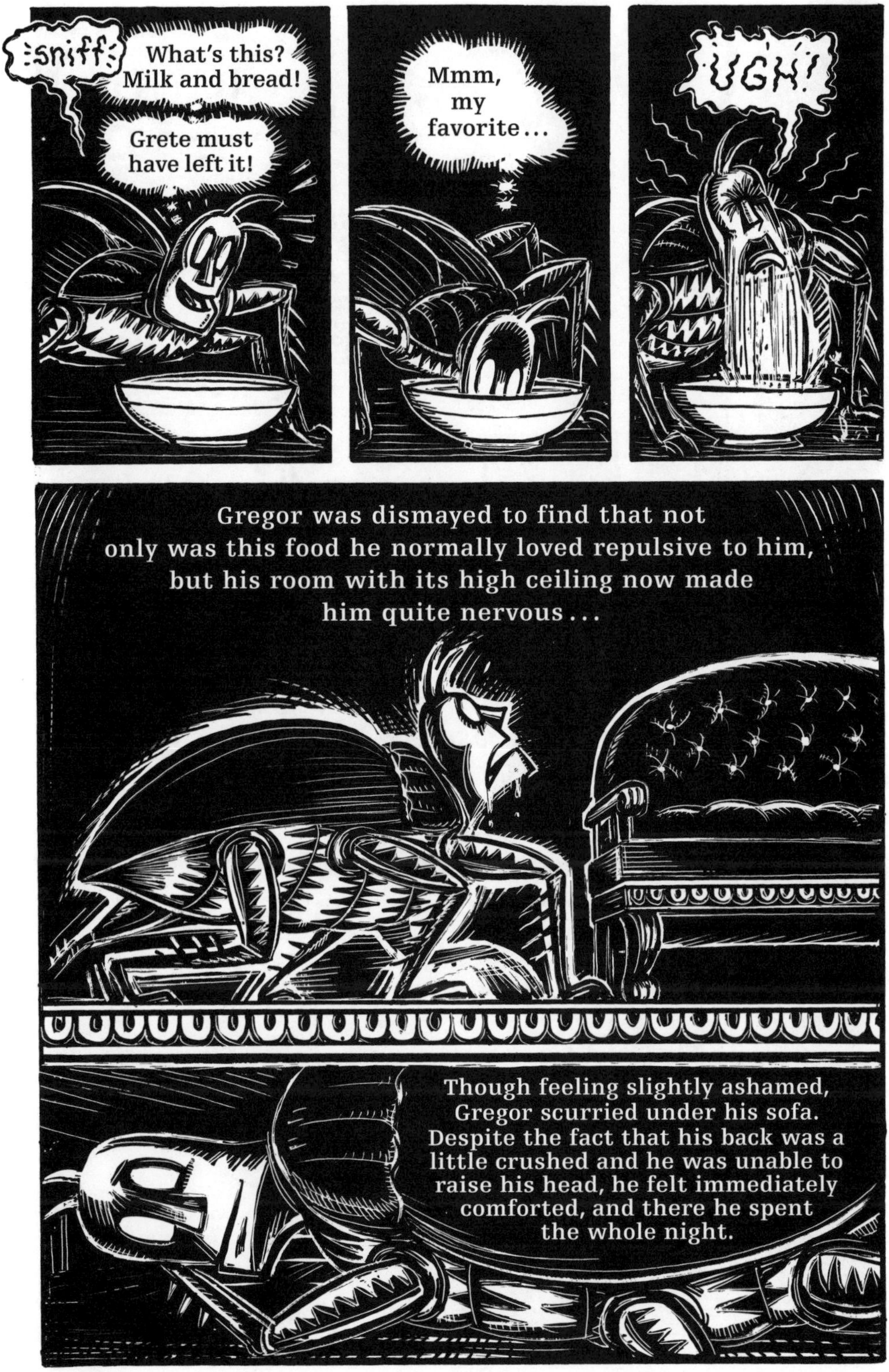
sniff
What's this? Milk and bread!
Grete must have left it!
Mmm, my favorite...
UGH!
Gregor was dismayed to find that not only was this food he normally loved repulsive to him, but his room with its high ceiling now made him quite nervous...
Though feeling slightly ashamed, Gregor scurried under his sofa. Despite the fact that his back was a little crushed and he was unable to raise his head, he felt immediately comforted, and there he spent the whole night.

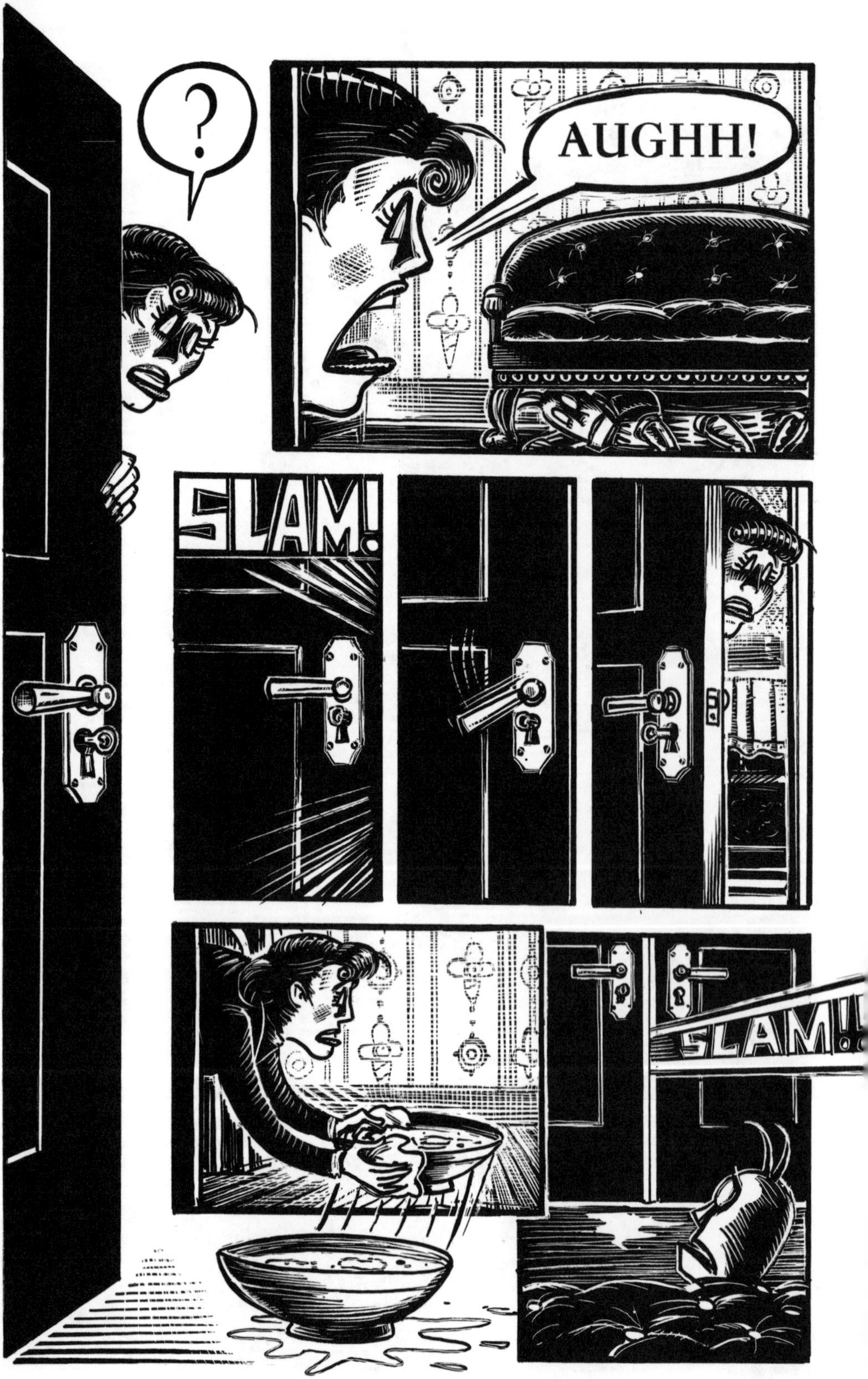
?
AUGHH!
SLAM!
SLAM!!

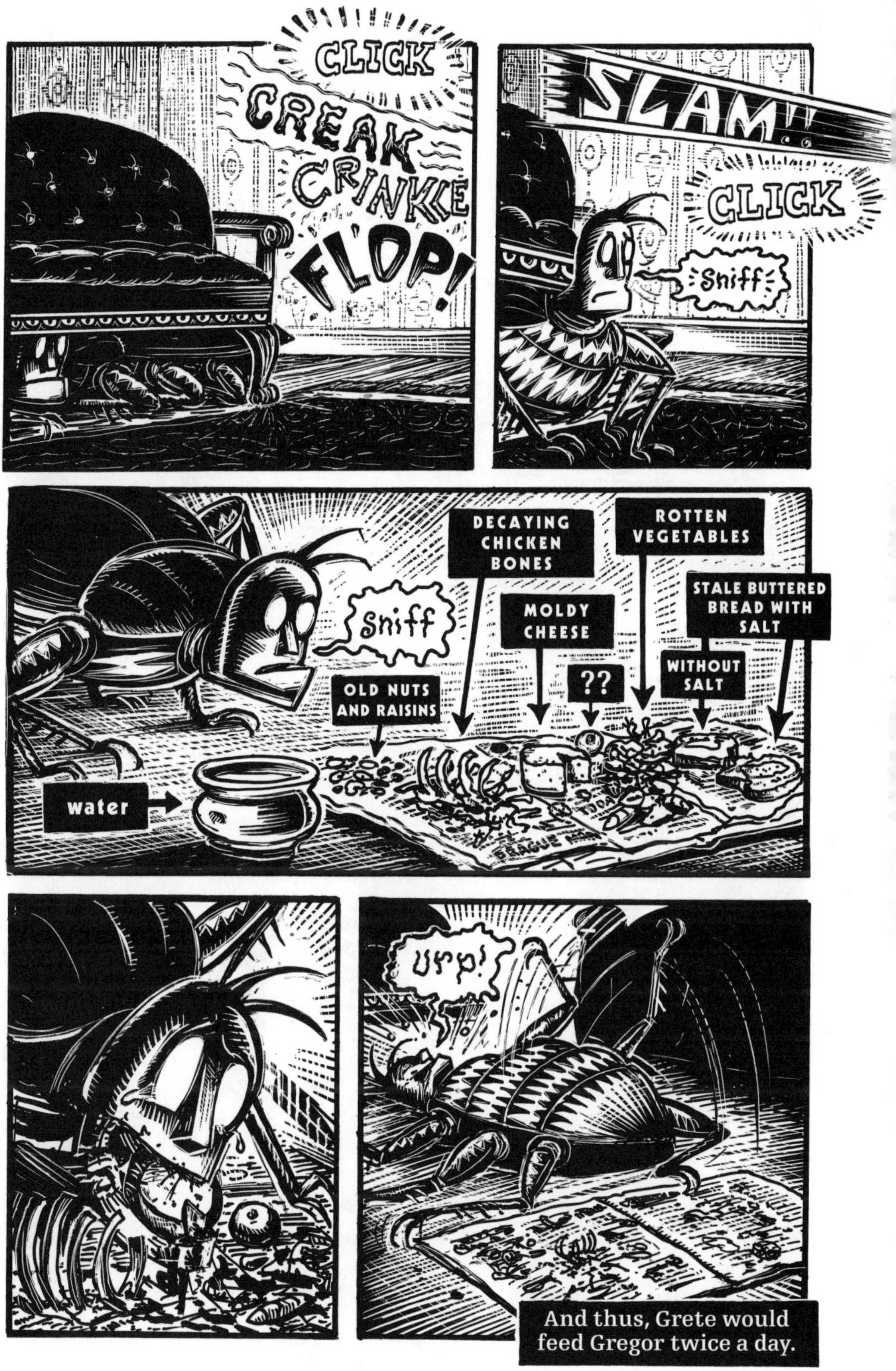
CLICK
CREAK
CRINKLE
FLOP!
SLAM!!
CLICK
Sniff
Sniff
DECAYING CHICKEN BONES
ROTTEN VEGETABLES
STALE BUTTERED BREAD WITH SALT
MOLDY CHEESE
??
WITHOUT SALT
OLD NUTS AND RAISINS
water
Urp!
And thus, Grete would feed Gregor twice a day.

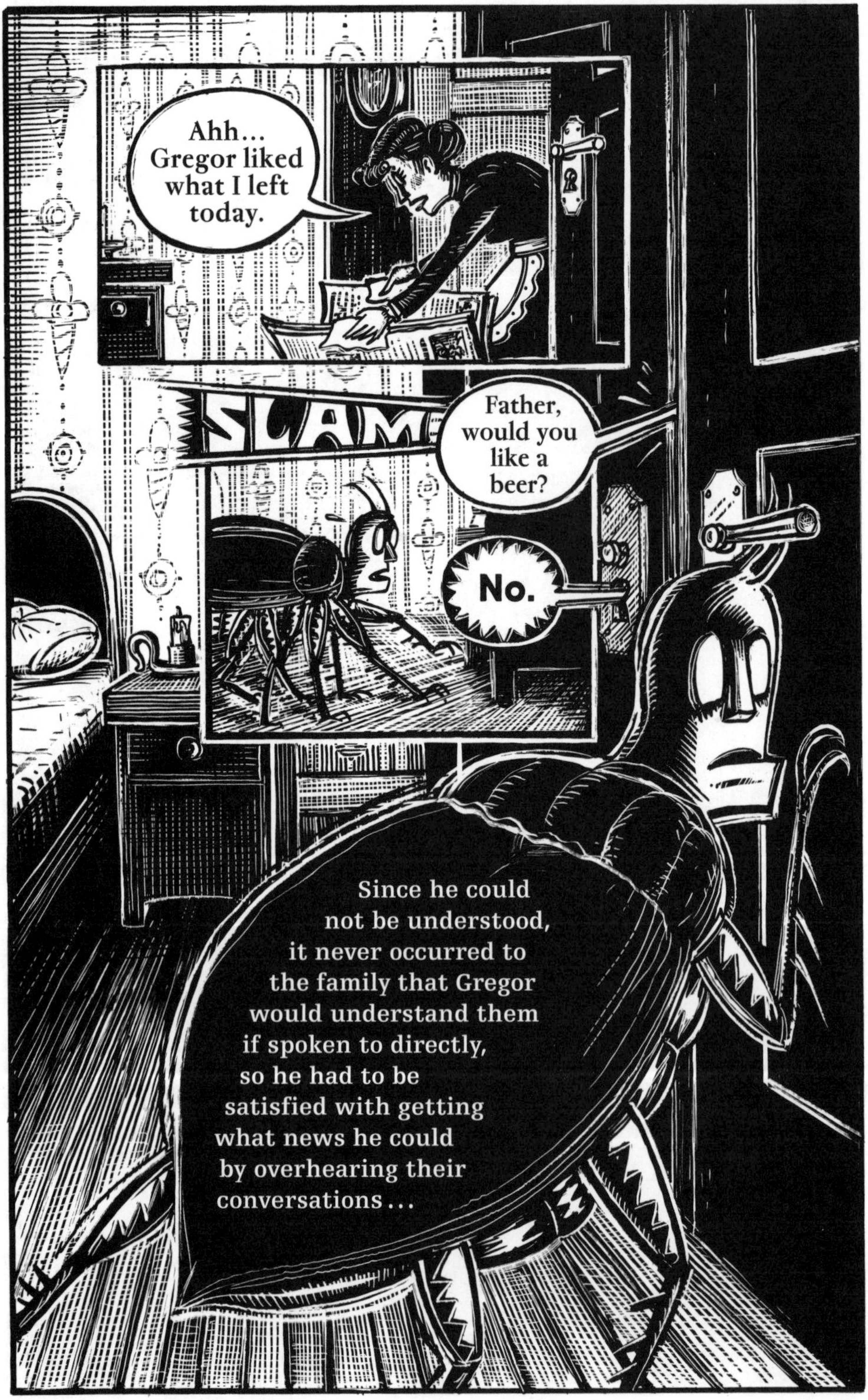
Ahh... Gregor liked what I left today.
SLAM
Father, would you like a beer?
No.
Since he could not be understood, it never occurred to the family that Gregor would understand them if spoken to directly, so he had to be satisfied with getting what news he could by overhearing their conversations...

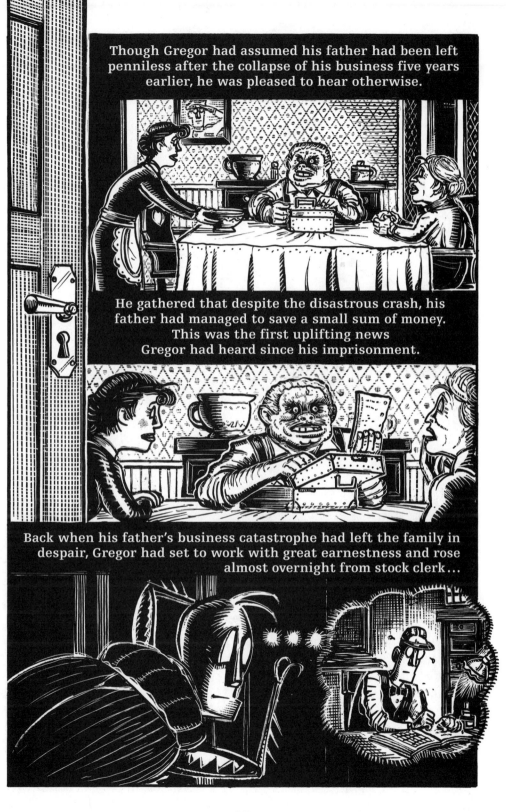

Though Gregor had assumed his father had been left penniless after the collapse of his business five years earlier, he was pleased to hear otherwise.

He gathered that despite the disastrous crash, his father had managed to save a small sum of money. This was the first uplifting news Gregor had heard since his imprisonment.

Back when his father's business catastrophe had left the family in despair, Gregor had set to work with great earnestness and rose almost overnight from stock clerk...

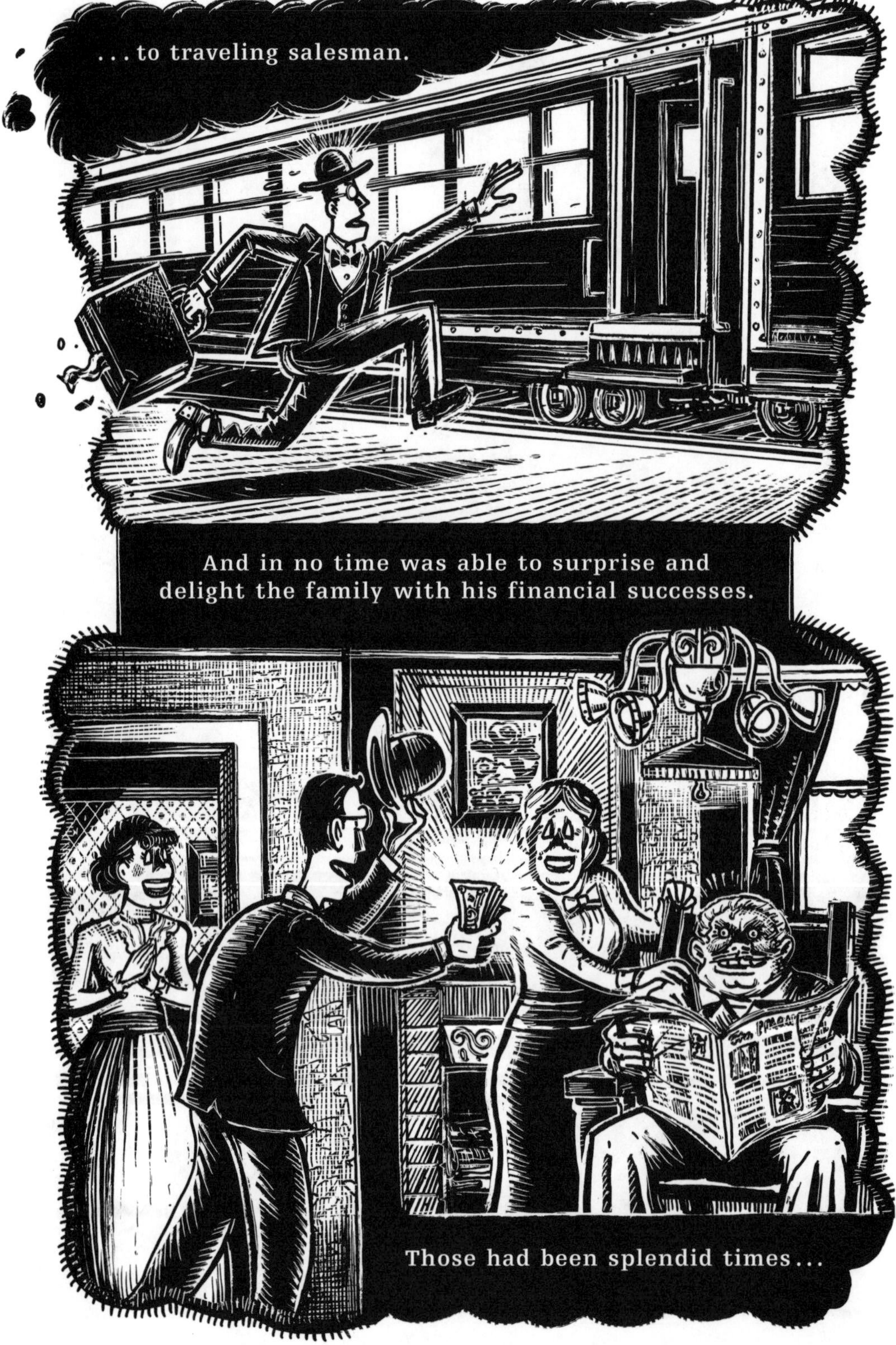
. . . to traveling salesman.
And in no time was able to surprise and delight the family with his financial successes.
Those had been splendid times . . .

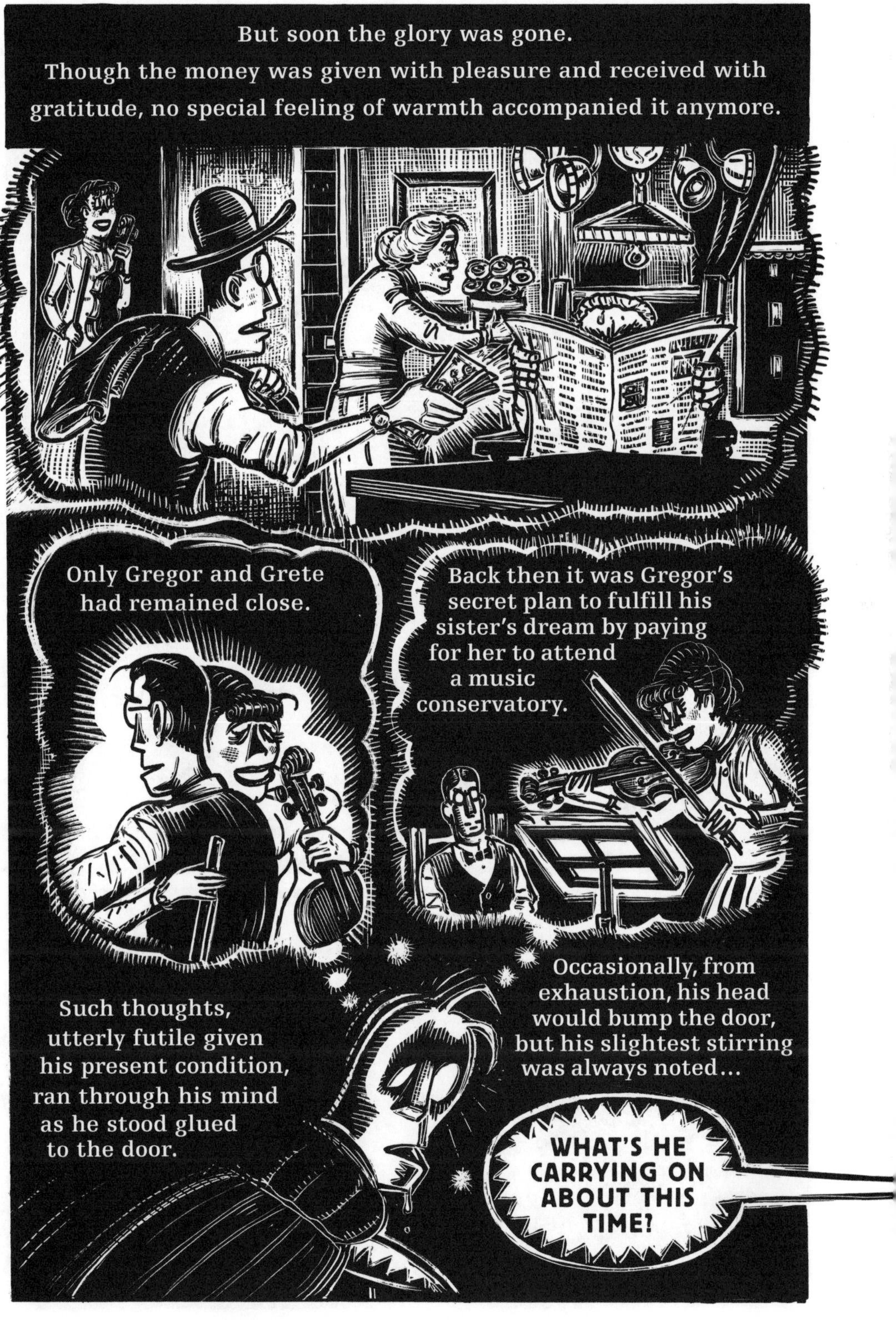
But soon the glory was gone.
Though the money was given with pleasure and received with gratitude, no special feeling of warmth accompanied it anymore.
Only Gregor and Grete had remained close.
Back then it was Gregor's secret plan to fulfill his sister's dream by paying for her to attend a music conservatory.
Such thoughts, utterly futile given his present condition, ran through his mind as he stood glued to the door.
Occasionally, from exhaustion, his head would bump the door, but his slightest stirring was always noted...
WHAT'S HE CARRYING ON ABOUT THIS TIME?

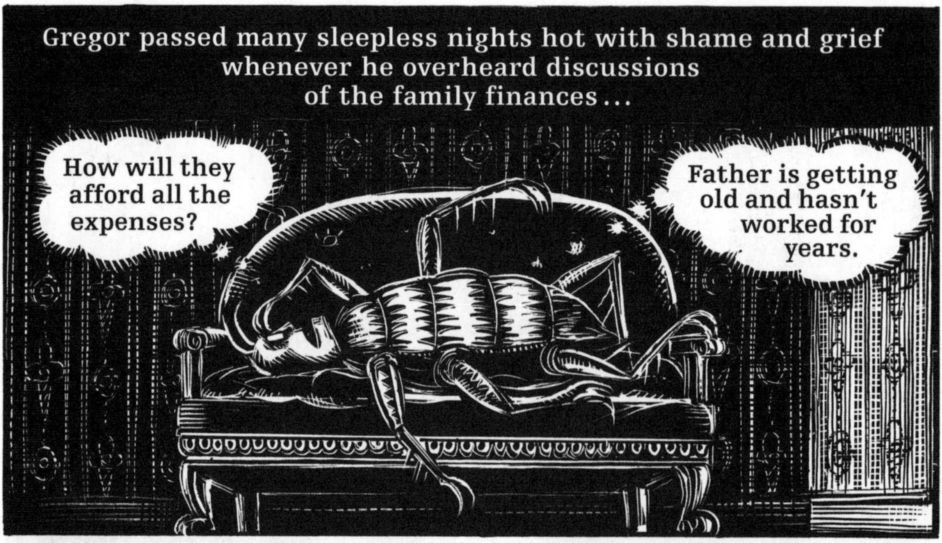
Gregor passed many sleepless nights hot with shame and grief
whenever he overheard discussions
of the family finances...
How will they afford all the expenses?
Father is getting old and hasn't worked for years.

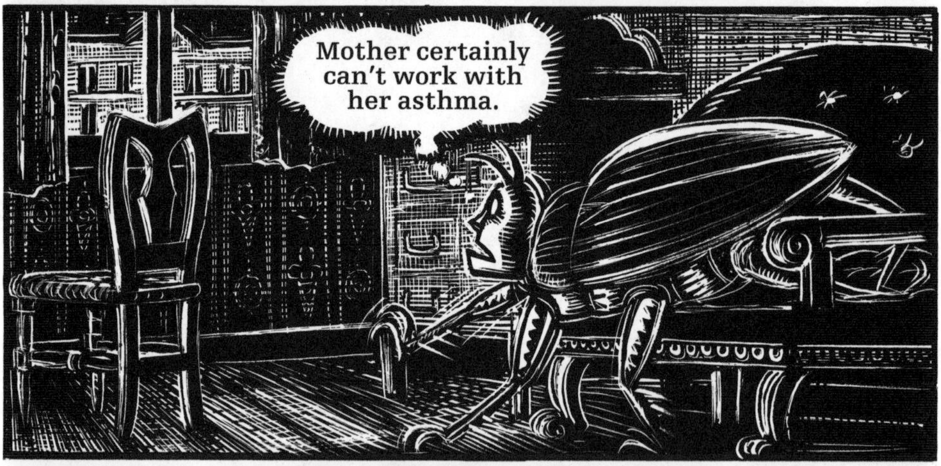
Mother certainly can't work with her asthma.

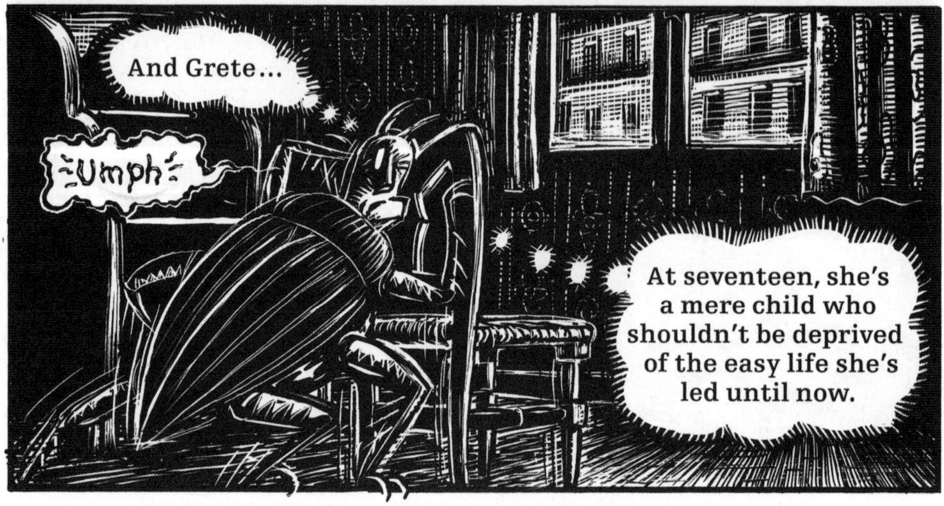
And Grete...
Umph
At seventeen, she's a mere child who shouldn't be deprived of the easy life she's led until now.

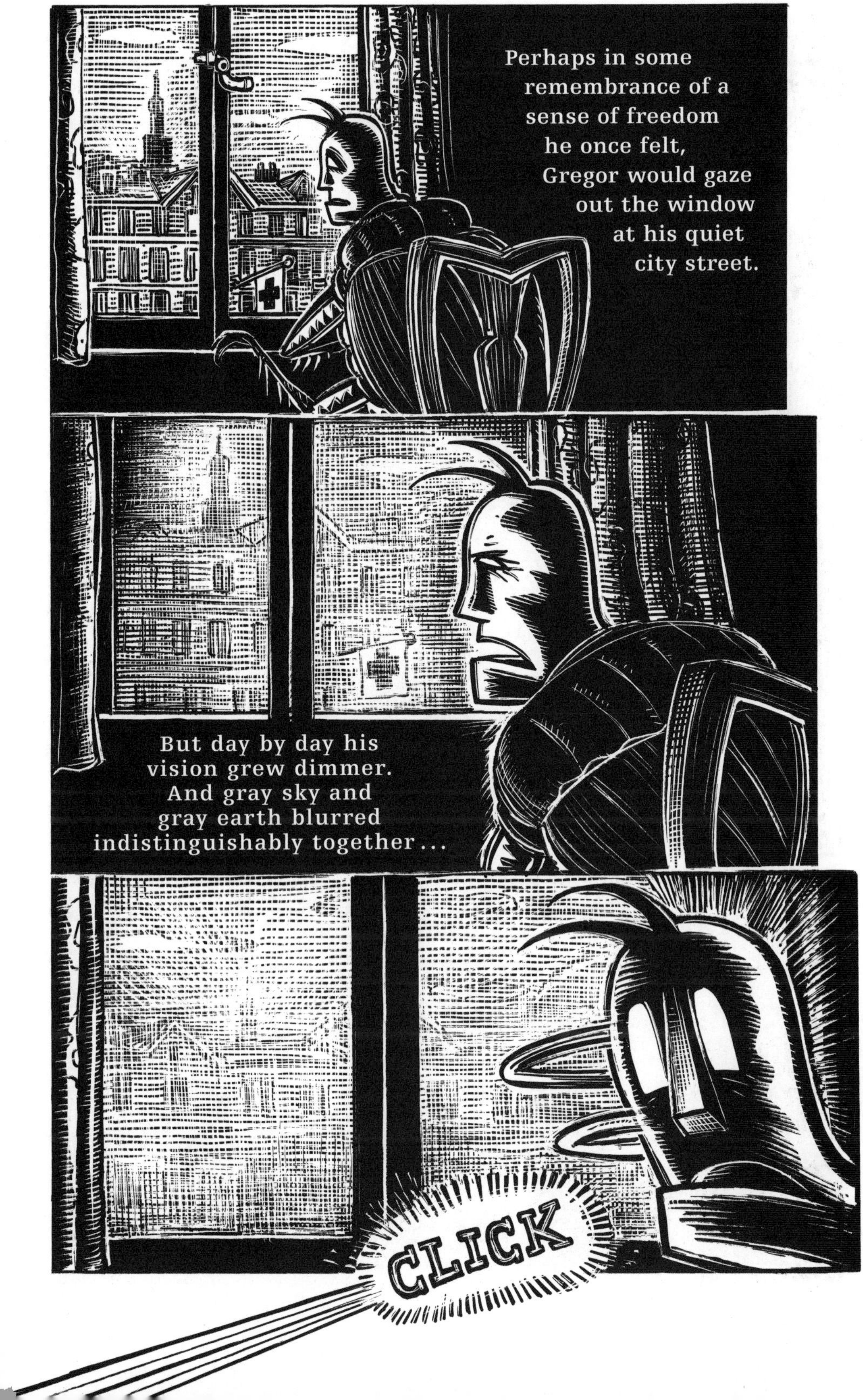
Perhaps in some remembrance of a sense of freedom he once felt, Gregor would gaze out the window at his quiet city street.
But day by day his vision grew dimmer. And gray sky and gray earth blurred indistinguishably together...
CLICK

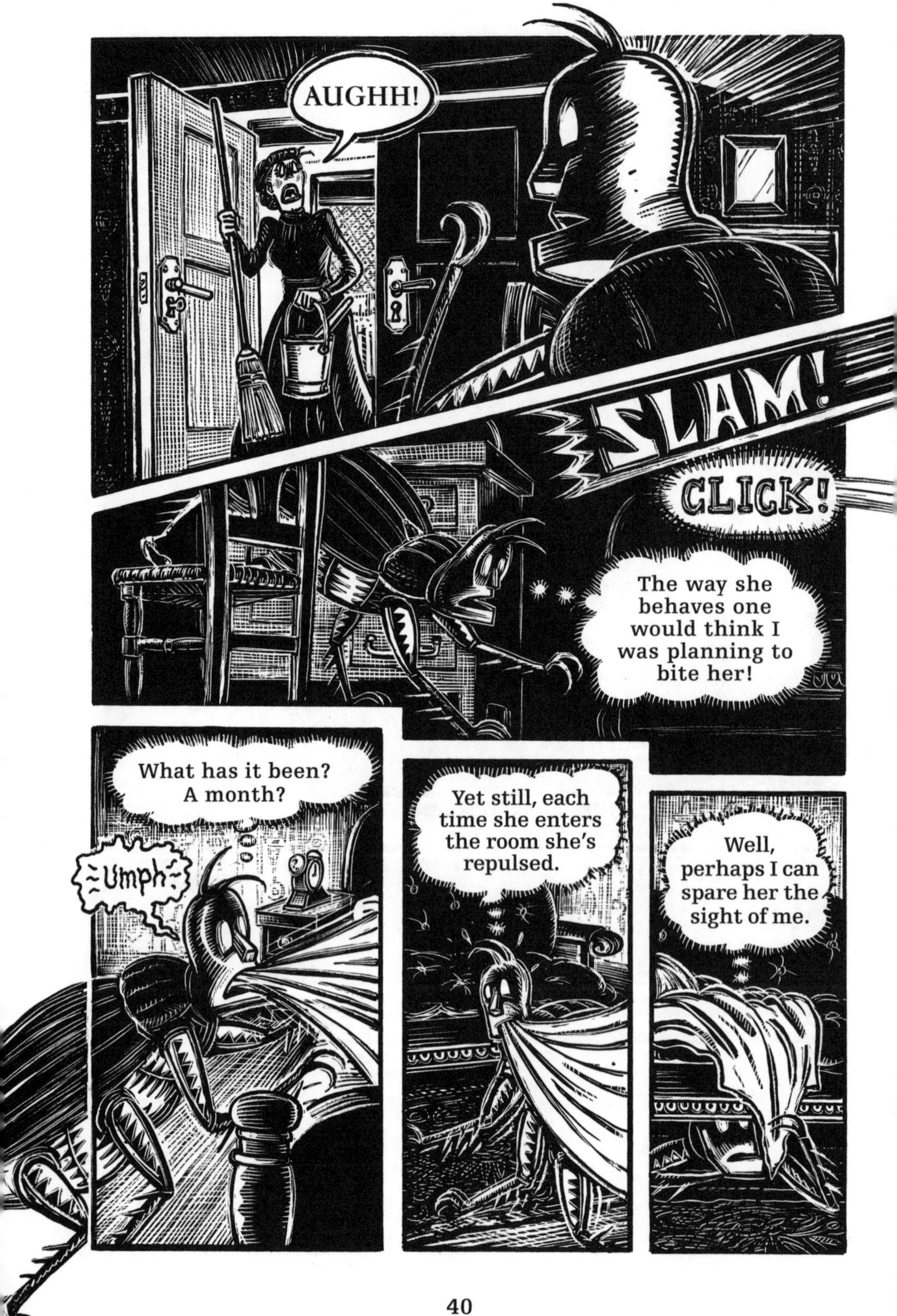
AUGHH!
SLAM!
CLICK!
The way she behaves one would think I was planning to bite her!
What has it been? A month?
Umph
Yet still, each time she enters the room she's repulsed.
Well, perhaps I can spare her the sight of me.

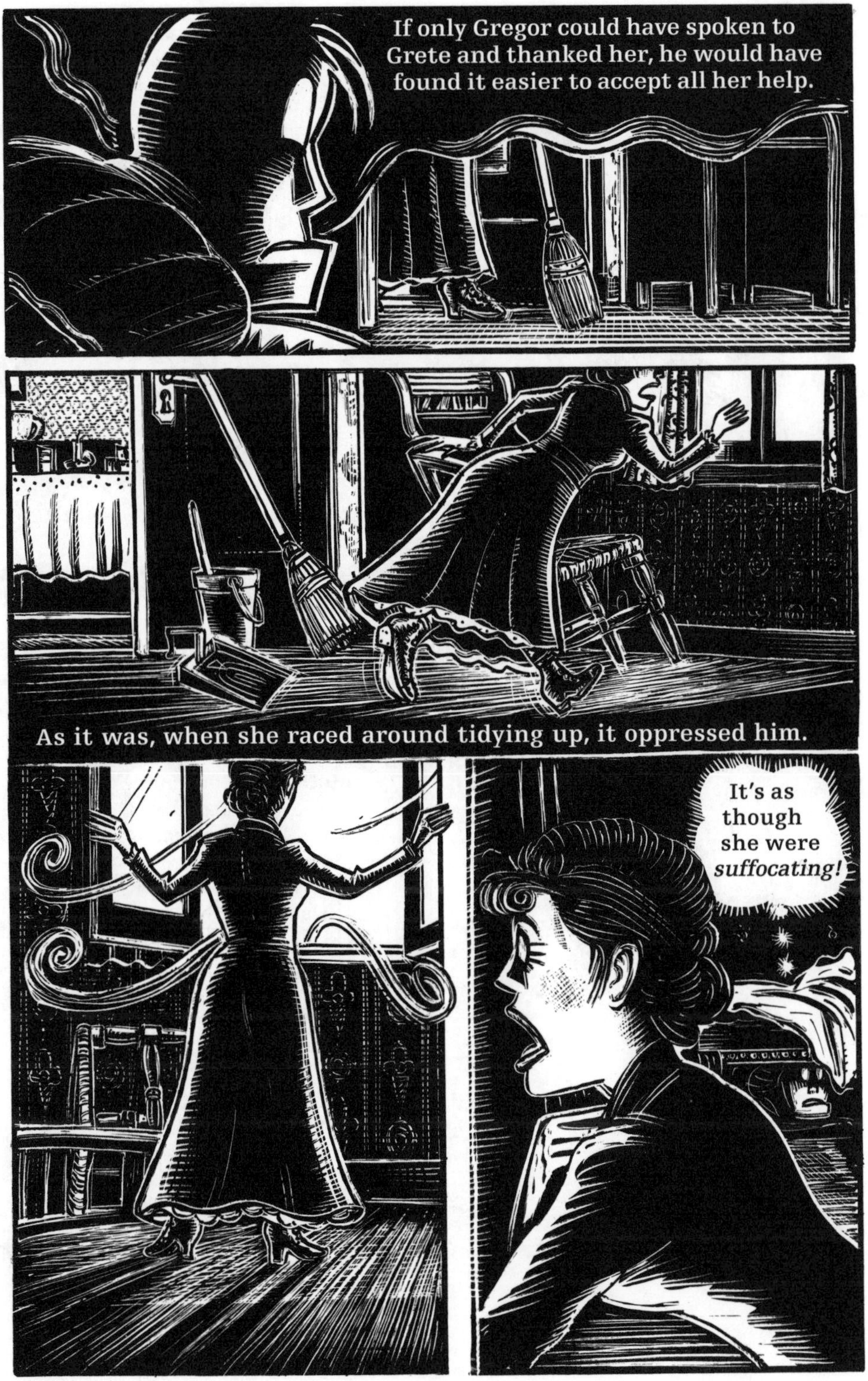
If only Gregor could have spoken to Grete and thanked her, he would have found it easier to accept all her help.
As it was, when she raced around tidying up, it oppressed him.
It's as though she were *suffocating!*

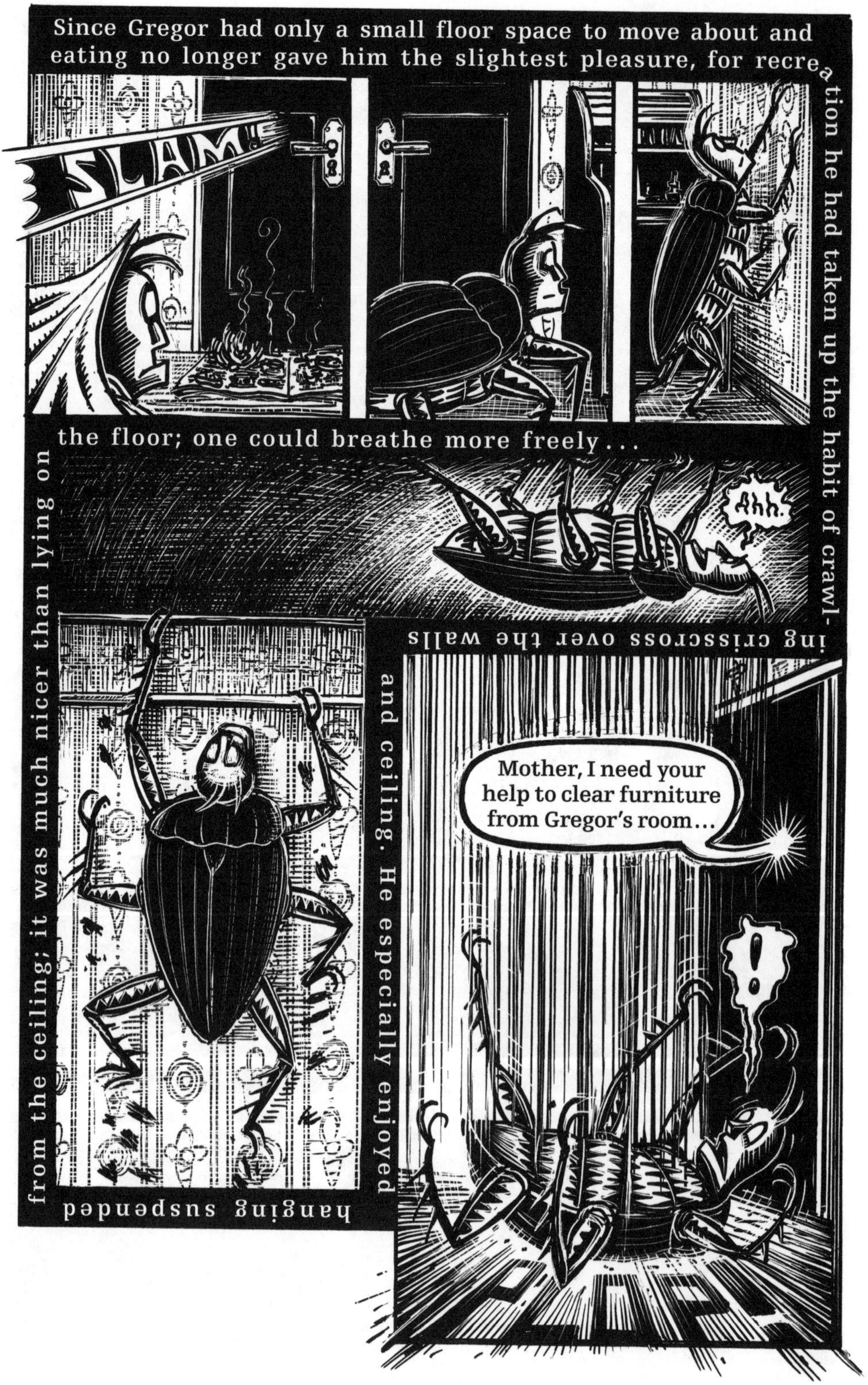

Since Gregor had only a small floor space to move about and eating no longer gave him the slightest pleasure, for recreation he had taken up the habit of crawling crisscross over the walls and ceiling. He especially enjoyed hanging suspended from the ceiling; it was much nicer than lying on the floor; one could breathe more freely...
SLAM!
Ahh.
Mother, I need your help to clear furniture from Gregor's room...
!

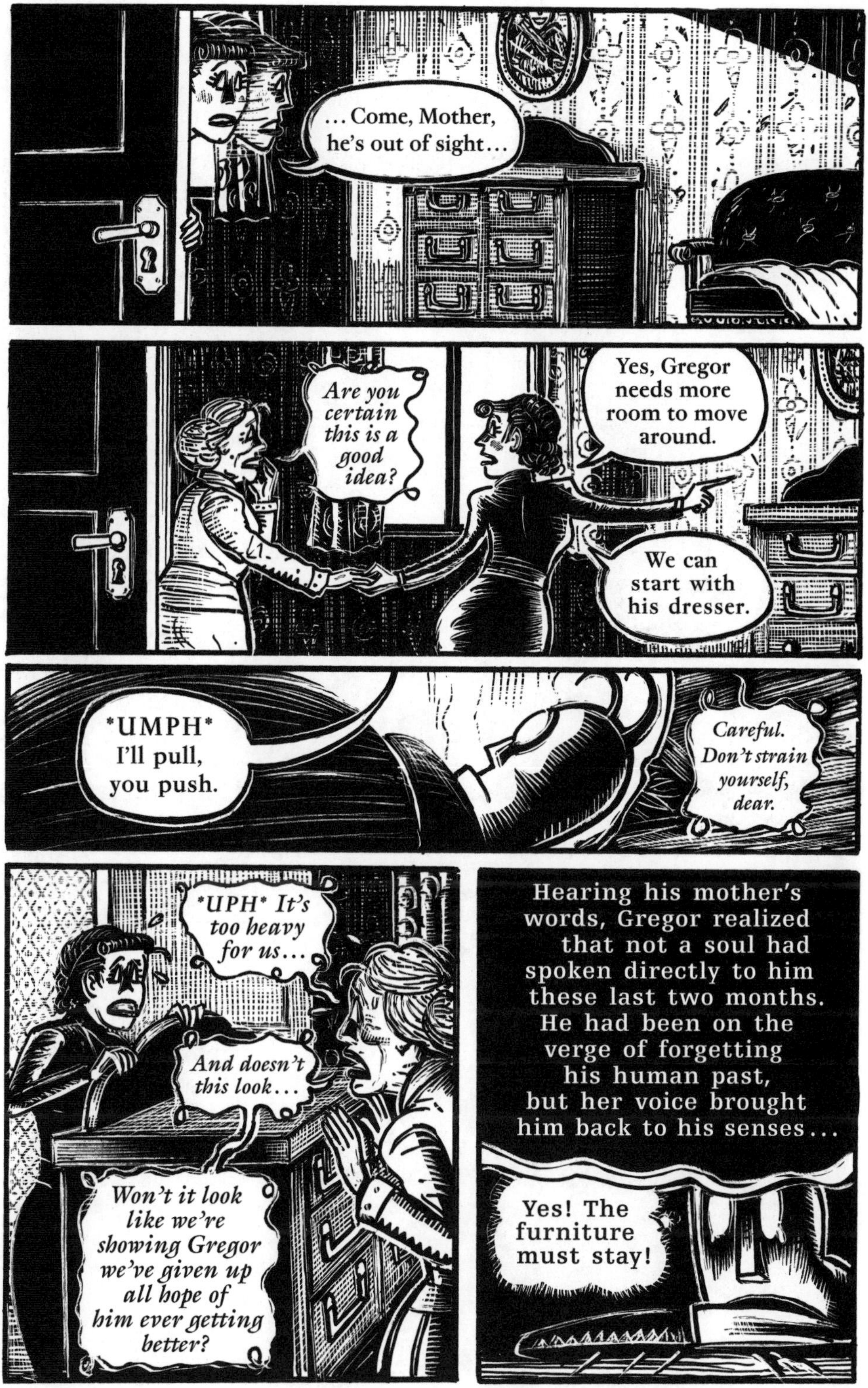

... Come, Mother, he's out of sight...
Are you certain this is a good idea?
Yes, Gregor needs more room to move around.
We can start with his dresser.
UMPH I'll pull, you push.
Careful. Don't strain yourself, dear.
UPH It's too heavy for us...
And doesn't this look...
Won't it look like we're showing Gregor we've given up all hope of him ever getting better?
Hearing his mother's words, Gregor realized that not a soul had spoken directly to him these last two months. He had been on the verge of forgetting his human past, but her voice brought him back to his senses...
Yes! The furniture must stay!

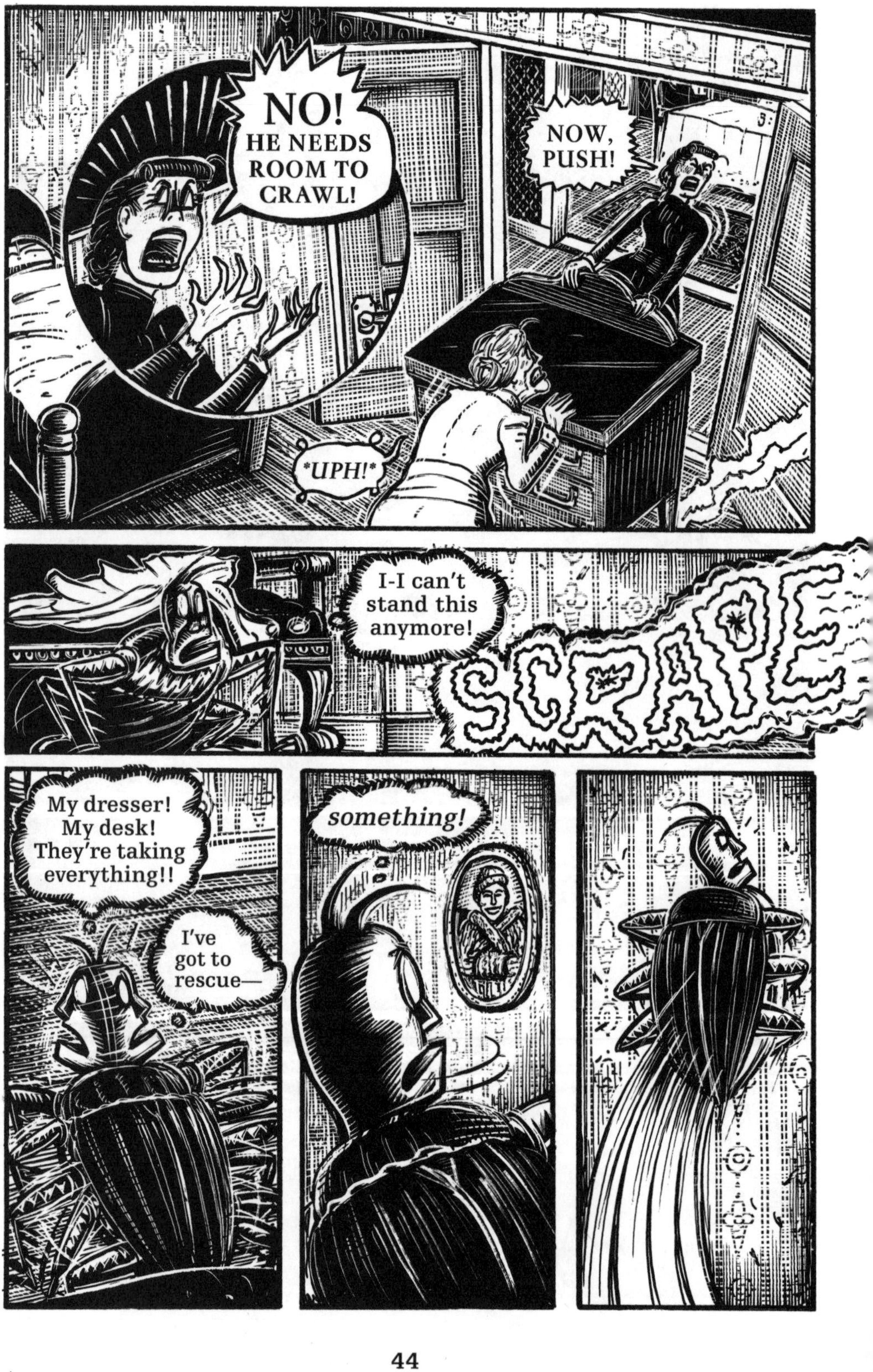
NO! HE NEEDS ROOM TO CRAWL!
NOW, PUSH!
UPH!
I-I can't stand this anymore!
SCRAPE
My dresser! My desk! They're taking everything!!
I've got to rescue—
something!

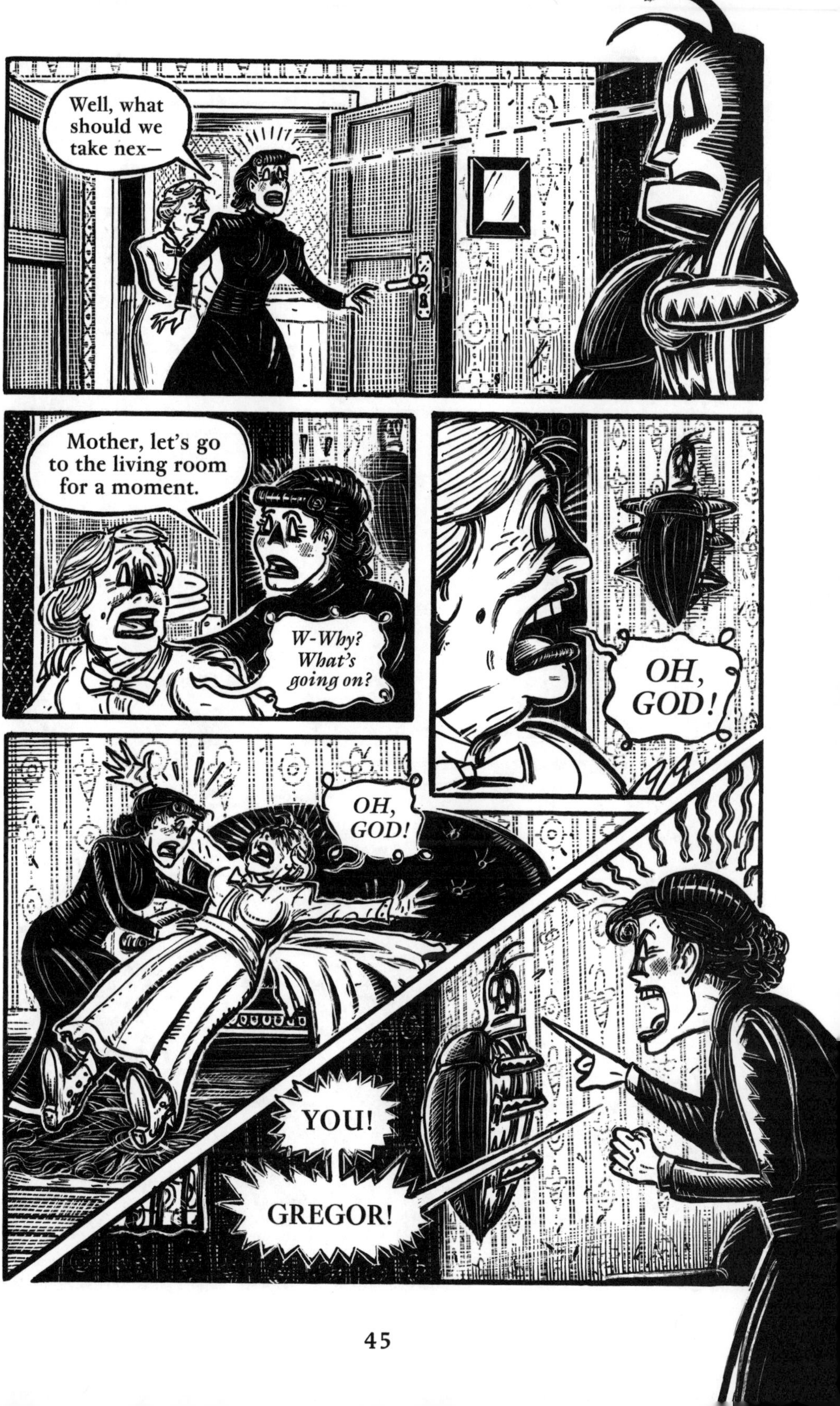

Well, what should we take nex—
Mother, let's go to the living room for a moment.
W-Why? What's going on?
OH, GOD!
OH, GOD!
YOU!
GREGOR!

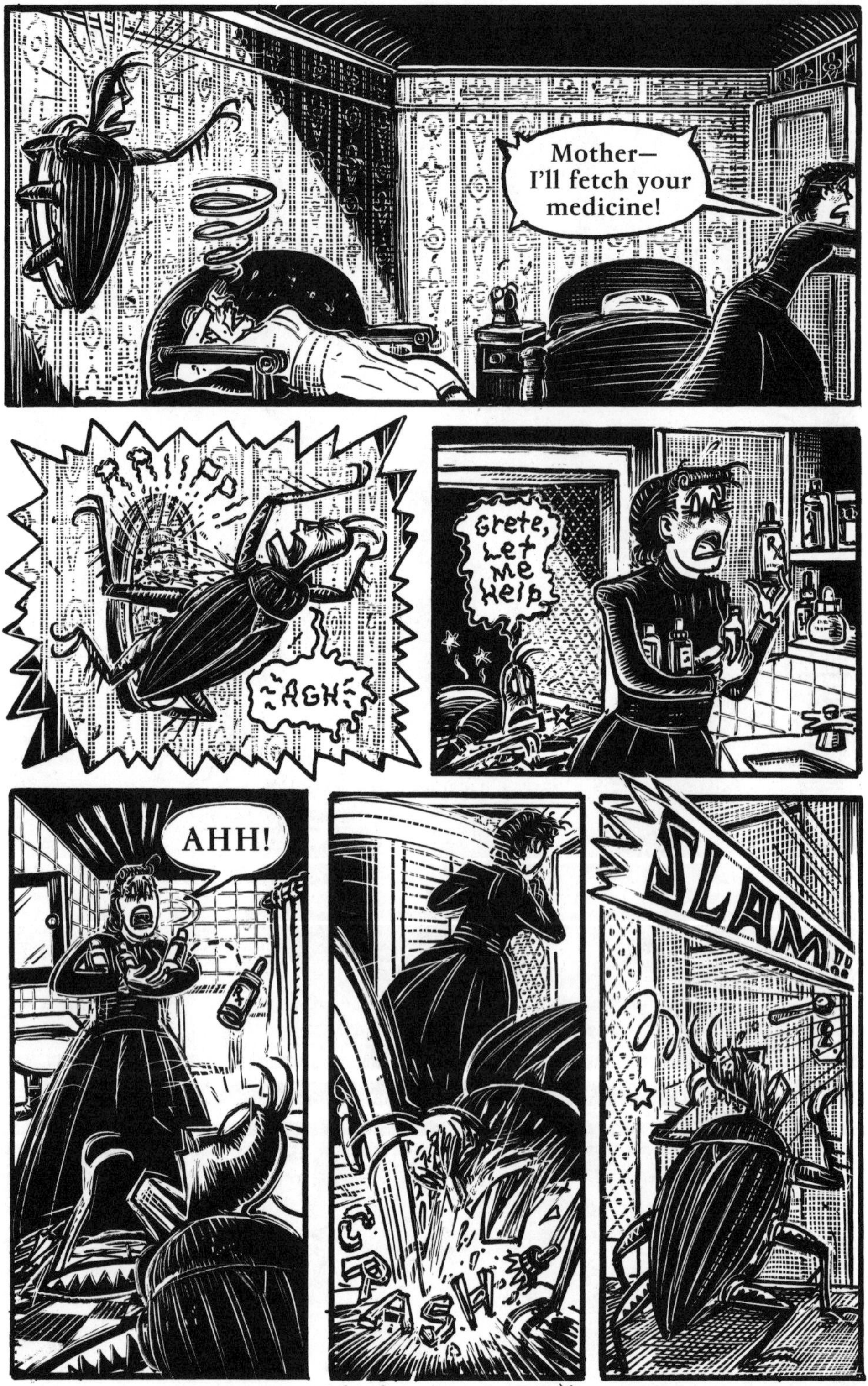
Mother—
I'll fetch your
medicine!
RRIIPP
AGH
Grete,
Let
me
Help
AHH!
CRASH
SLAM!!

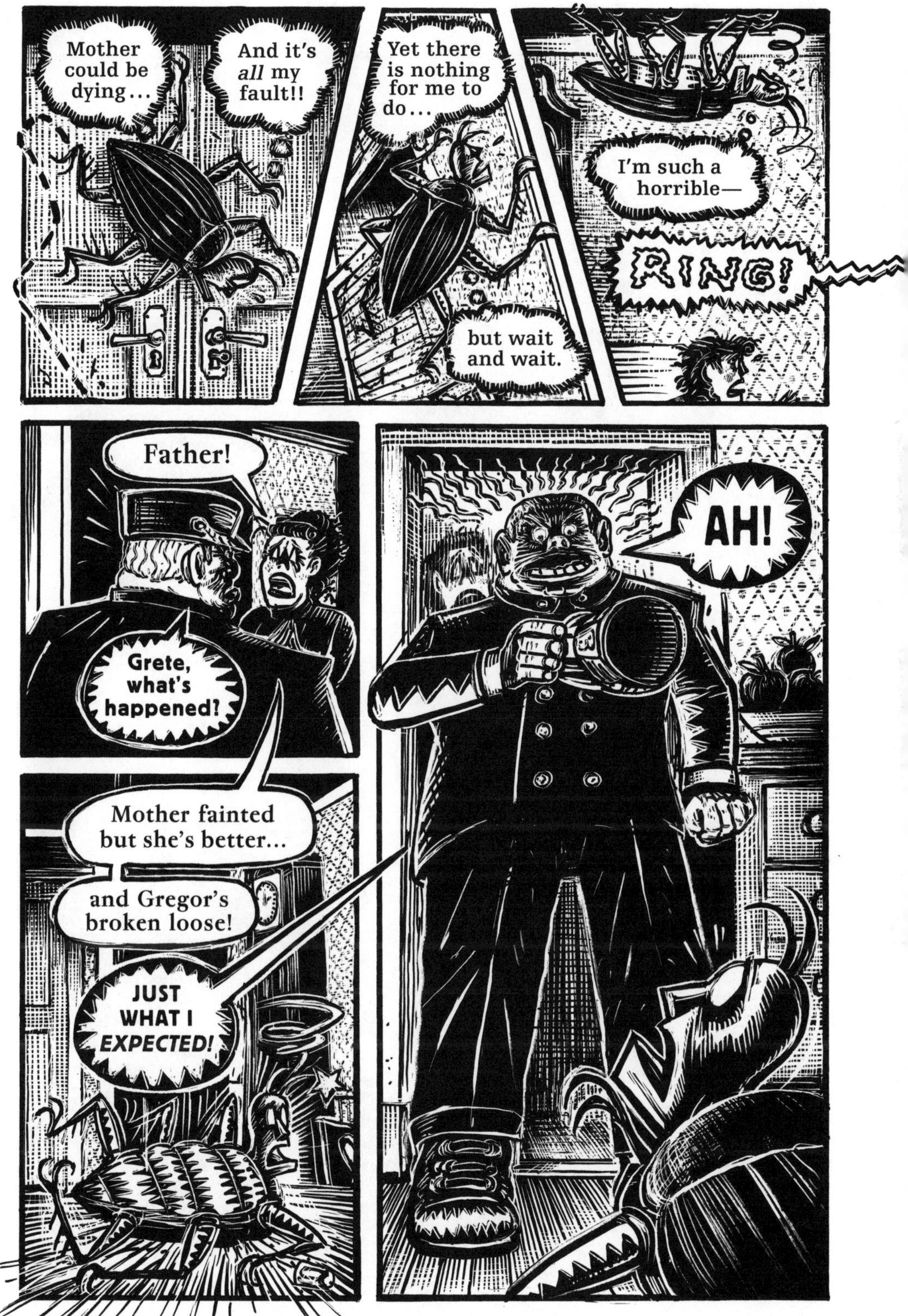
Mother could be dying...
And it's *all* my fault!!
Yet there is nothing for me to do...
but wait and wait.
I'm such a horrible—
RING!
Father!
Grete, what's happened?
AH!
Mother fainted but she's better...
and Gregor's broken loose!
JUST WHAT I *EXPECTED!*

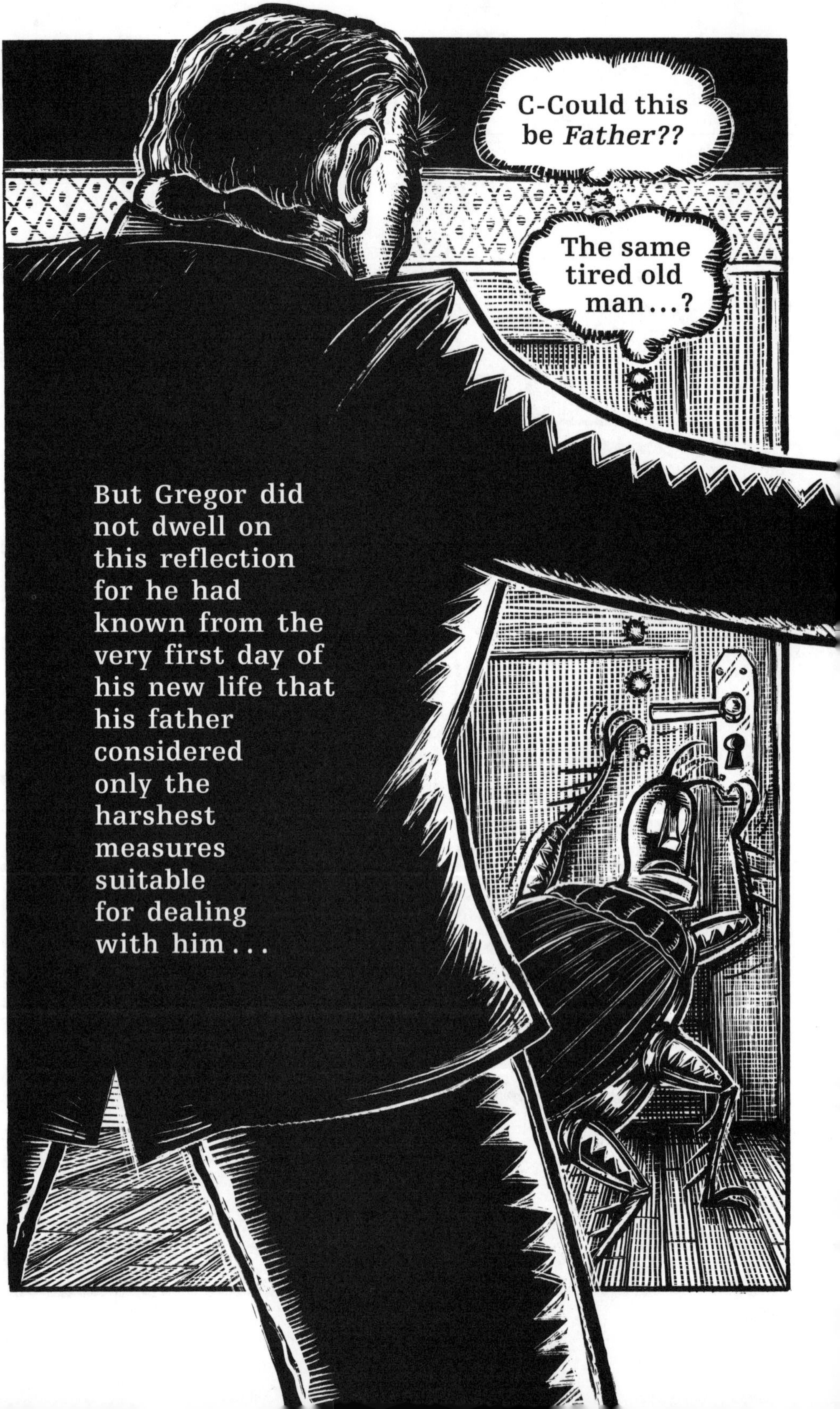

C-Could this be *Father??*
The same tired old man...?
But Gregor did not dwell on this reflection for he had known from the very first day of his new life that his father considered only the harshest measures suitable for dealing with him...

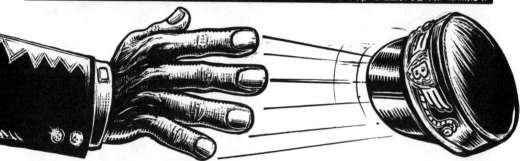

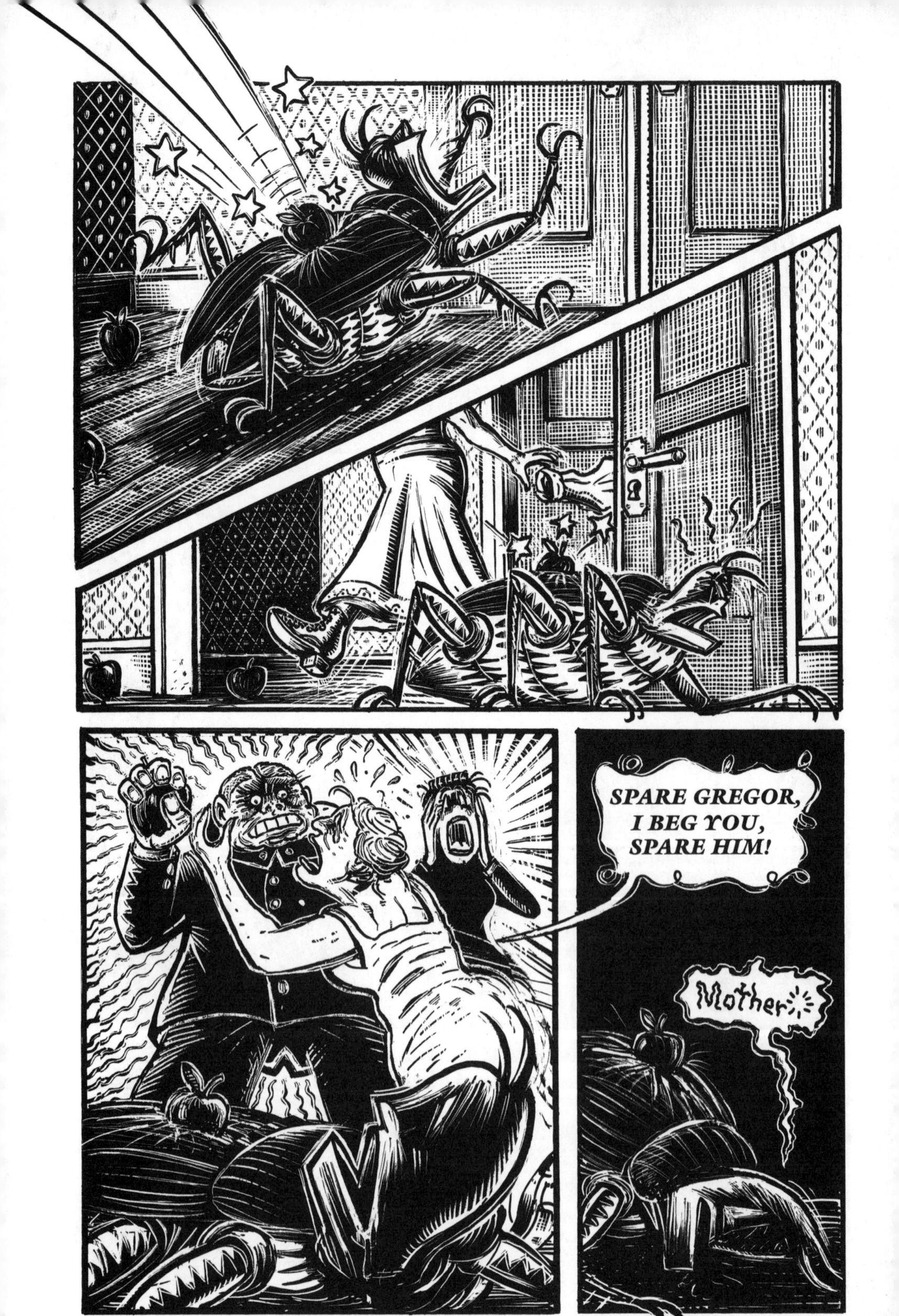
SPARE GREGOR,
I BEG YOU,
SPARE HIM!
Mother

III

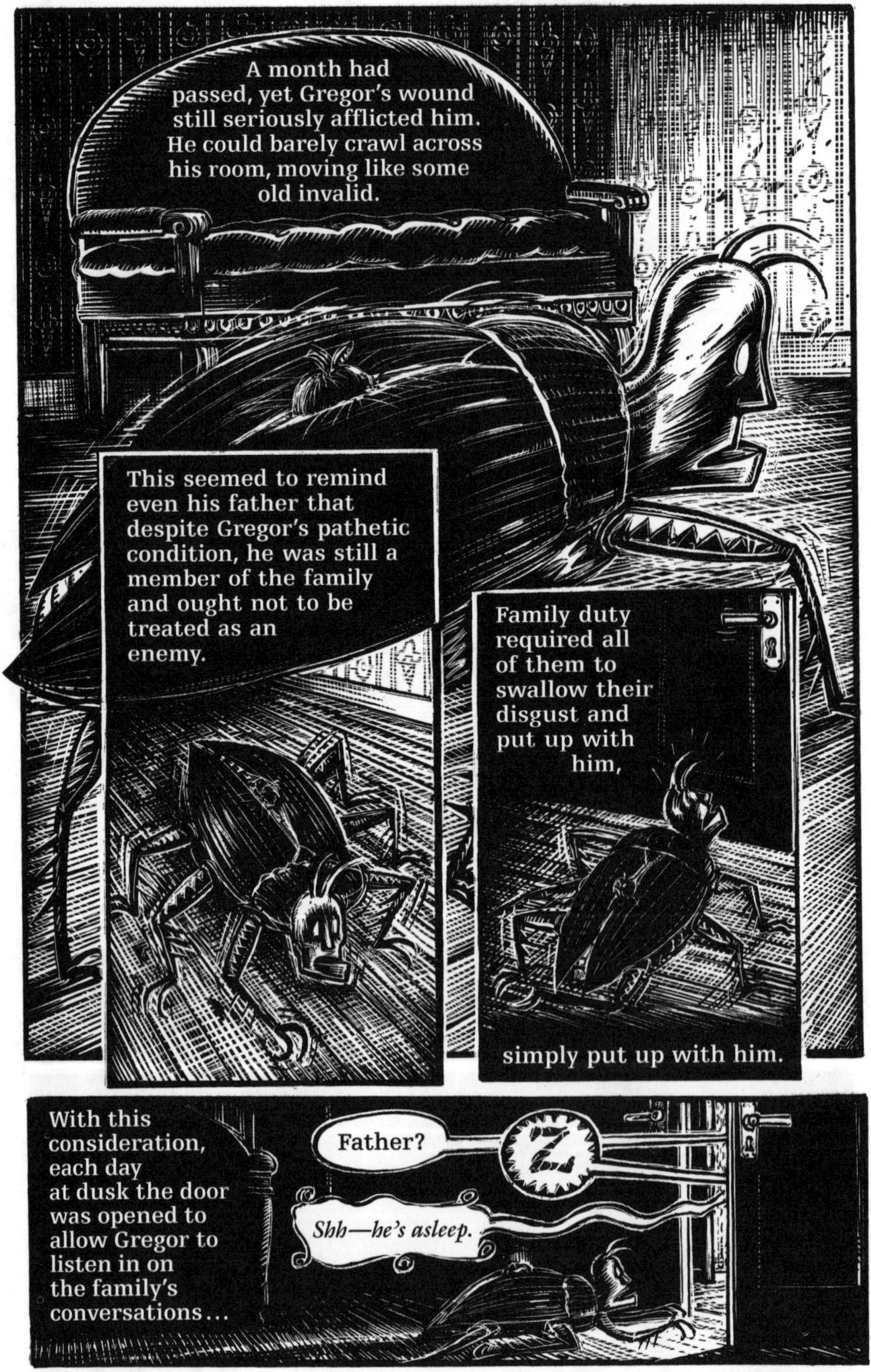
A month had passed, yet Gregor's wound still seriously afflicted him. He could barely crawl across his room, moving like some old invalid.
This seemed to remind even his father that despite Gregor's pathetic condition, he was still a member of the family and ought not to be treated as an enemy.
Family duty required all of them to swallow their disgust and put up with him,
simply put up with him.
With this consideration, each day at dusk the door was opened to allow Gregor to listen in on the family's conversations...
Father?
Z
Shh—he's asleep.

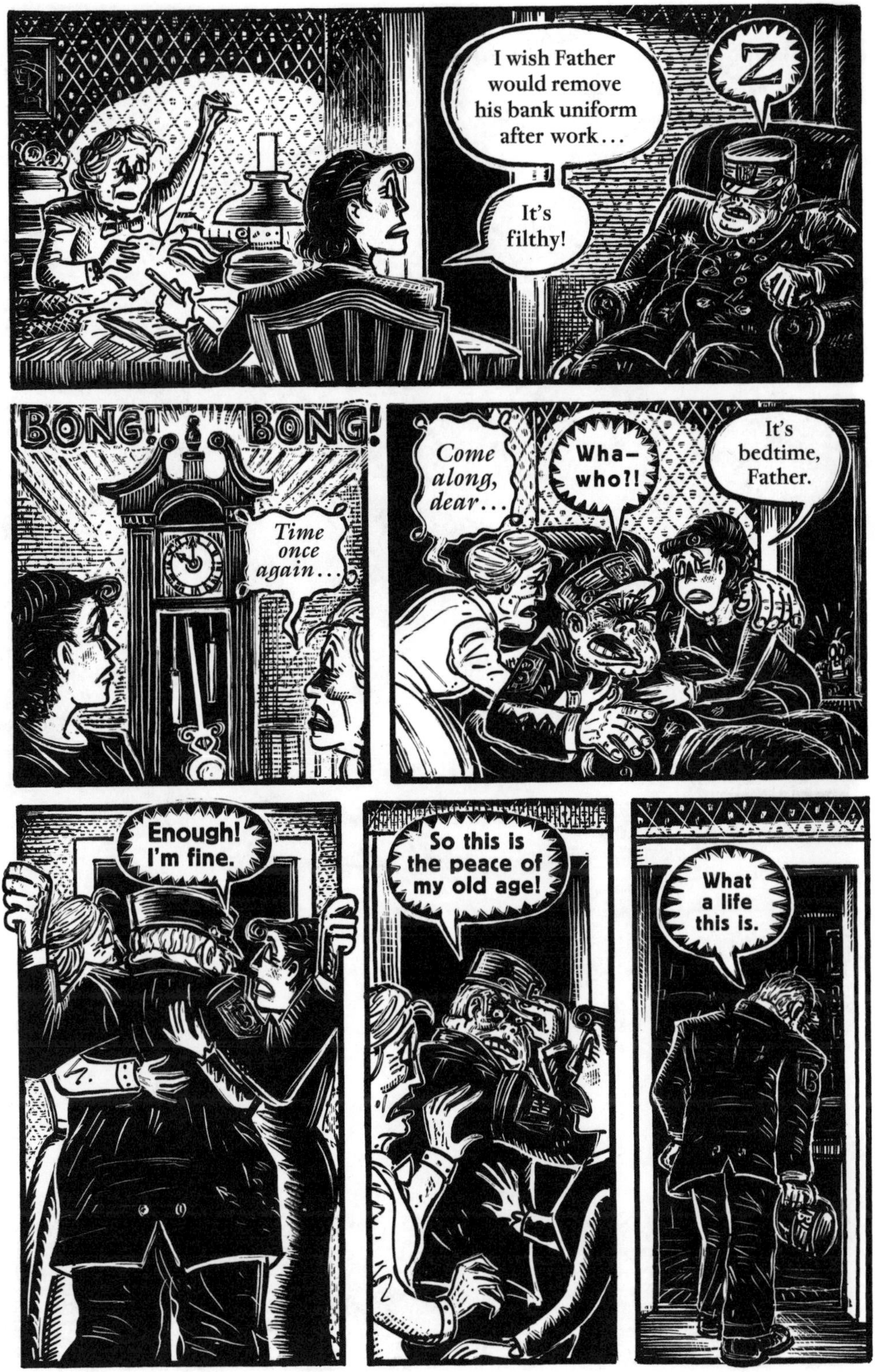
I wish Father would remove his bank uniform after work…
It's filthy!
Z
BONG! BONG!
Time once again…
Come along, dear…
Wha—who?!
It's bedtime, Father.
Enough! I'm fine.
So this is the peace of my old age!
What a life this is.

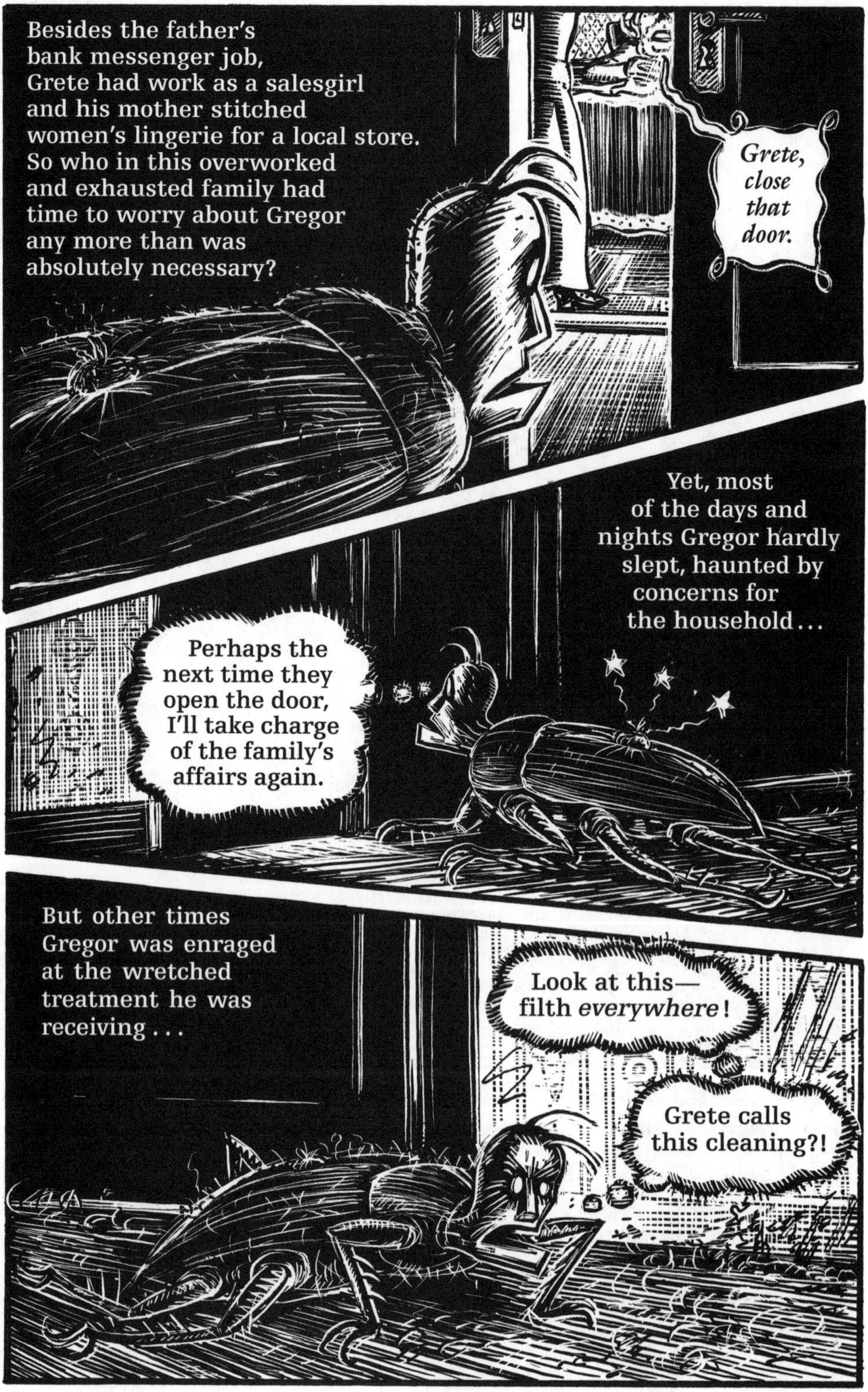
Besides the father's bank messenger job, Grete had work as a salesgirl and his mother stitched women's lingerie for a local store. So who in this overworked and exhausted family had time to worry about Gregor any more than was absolutely necessary?
Grete, close that door.
Yet, most of the days and nights Gregor hardly slept, haunted by concerns for the household...
Perhaps the next time they open the door, I'll take charge of the family's affairs again.
But other times Gregor was enraged at the wretched treatment he was receiving...
Look at this— filth *everywhere*!
Grete calls this cleaning?!

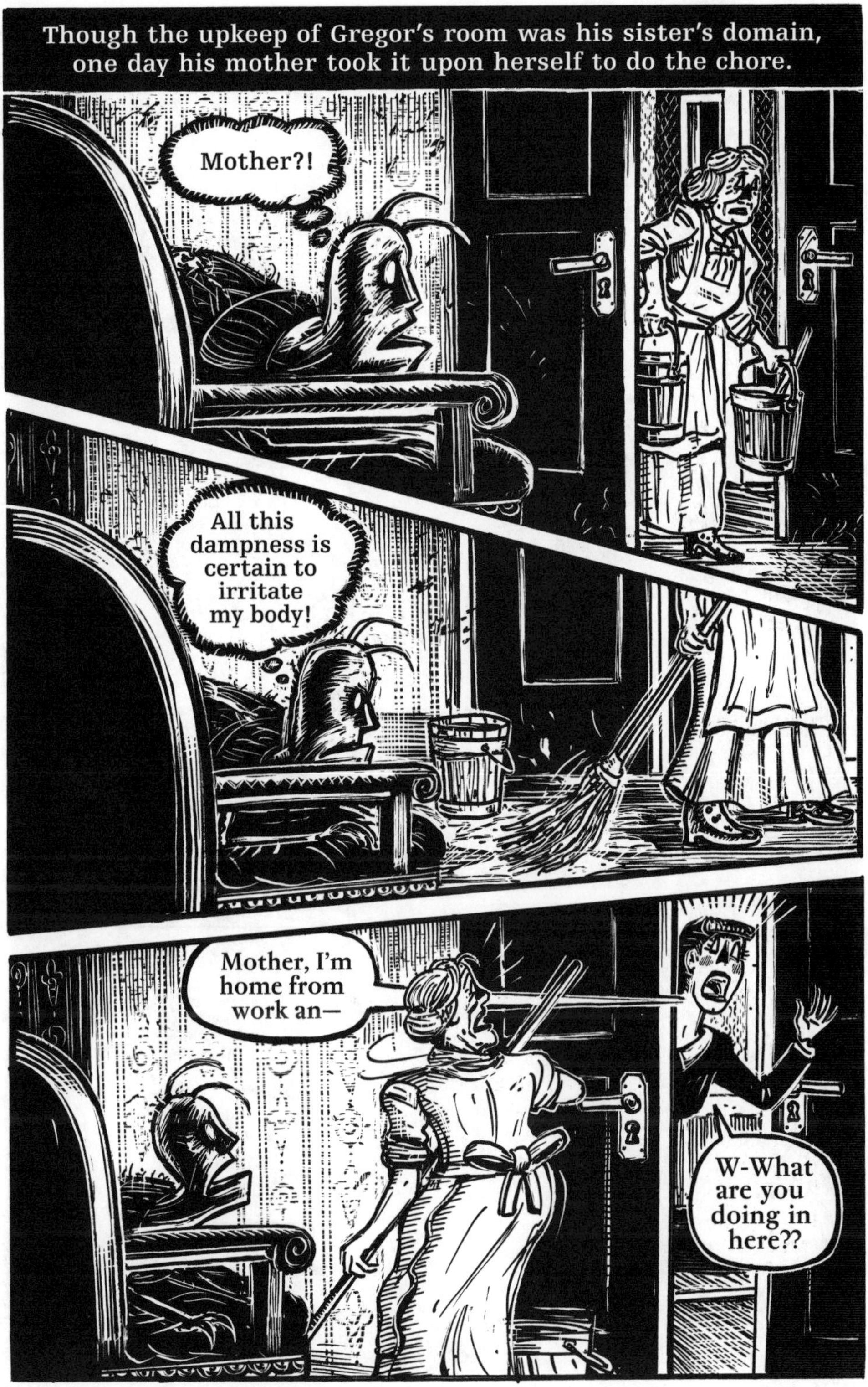
Though the upkeep of Gregor's room was his sister's domain, one day his mother took it upon herself to do the chore.
Mother?!
All this dampness is certain to irritate my body!
Mother, I'm home from work an—
W-What are you doing in here??

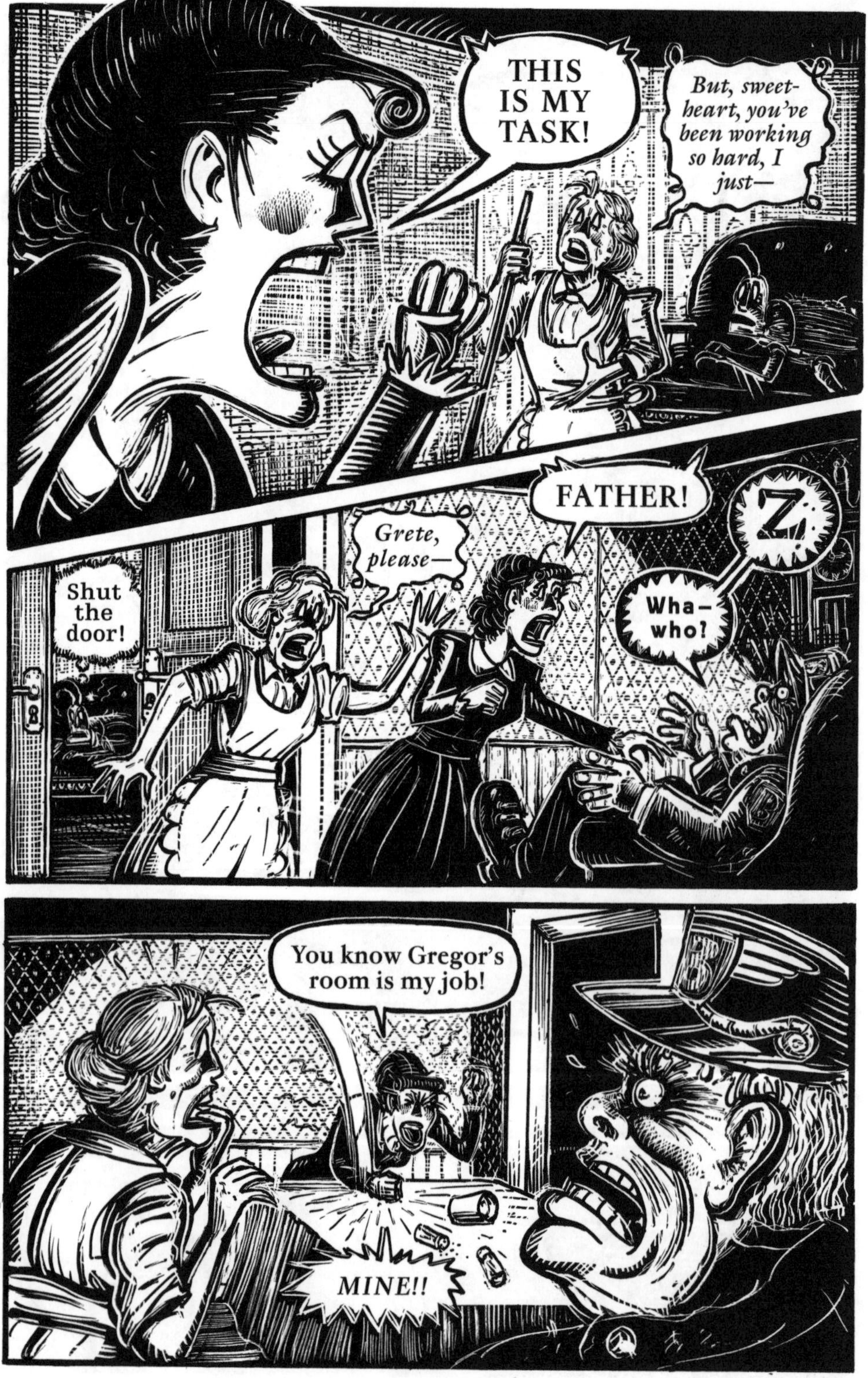
THIS IS MY TASK!
But, sweetheart, you've been working so hard, I just—
FATHER!
Z
Grete, please—
Shut the door!
Wha—who?
You know Gregor's room is my job!
MINE!!

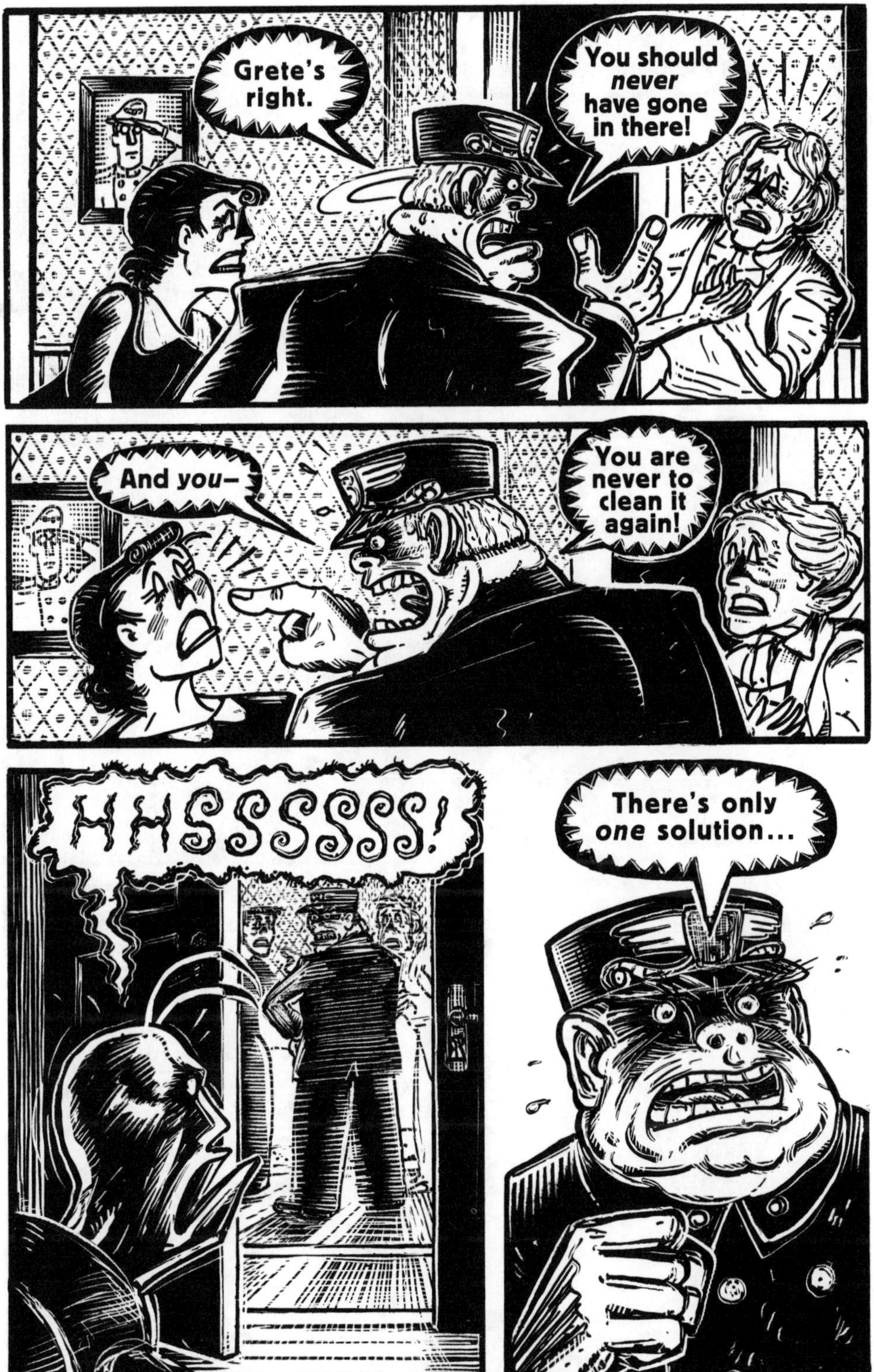
Grete's right.
You should *never* have gone in there!
And *you*–
You are never to clean it again!
HHSSSSSS!
There's only *one* solution...

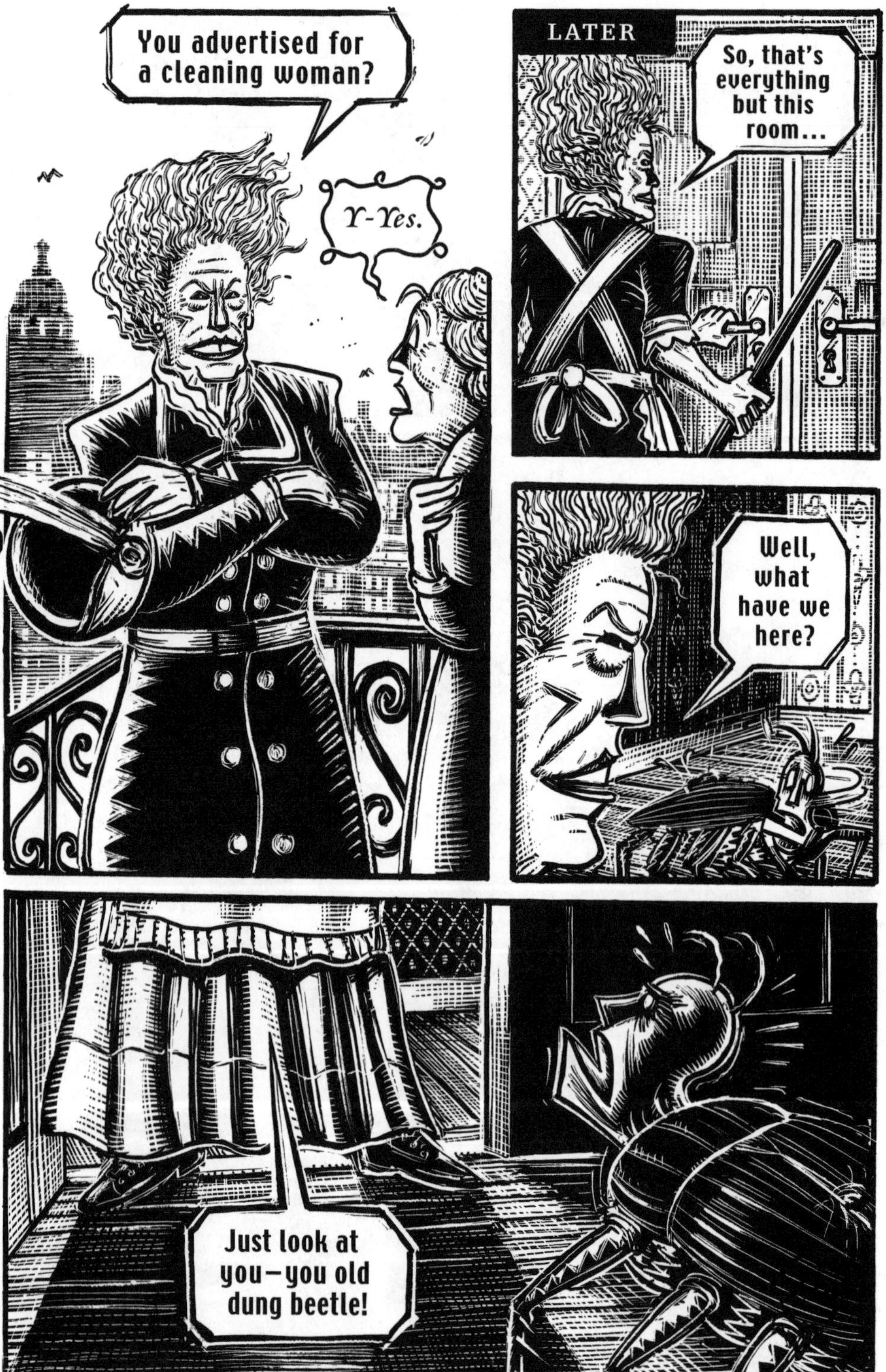
You advertised for a cleaning woman?
Y-Yes.
LATER
So, that's everything but this room...
Well, what have we here?
Just look at you—you old dung beetle!

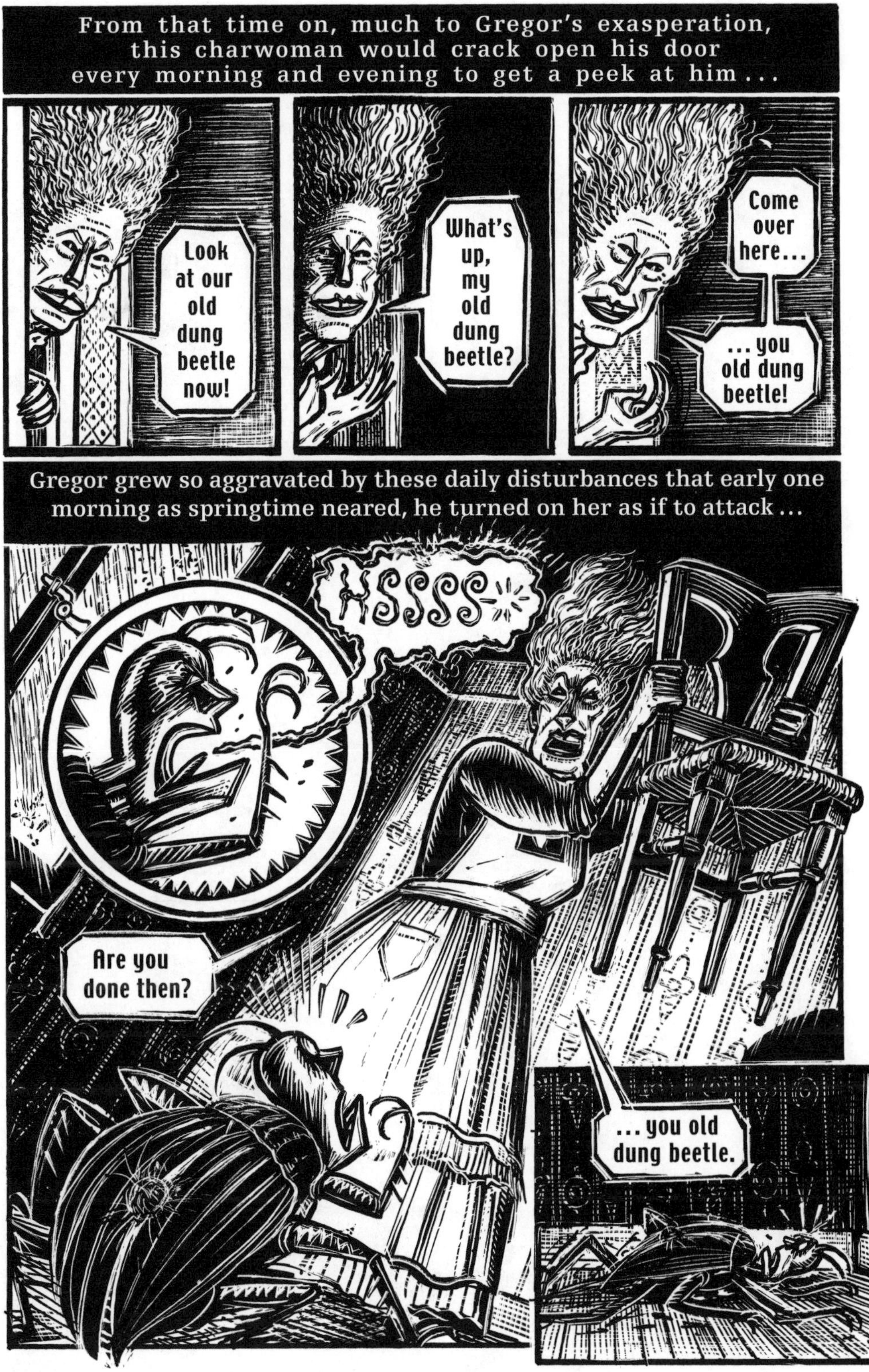
From that time on, much to Gregor's exasperation, this charwoman would crack open his door every morning and evening to get a peek at him...
Look at our old dung beetle now!
What's up, my old dung beetle?
Come over here...
...you old dung beetle!
Gregor grew so aggravated by these daily disturbances that early one morning as springtime neared, he turned on her as if to attack...
HSSSS
Are you done then?
...you old dung beetle.

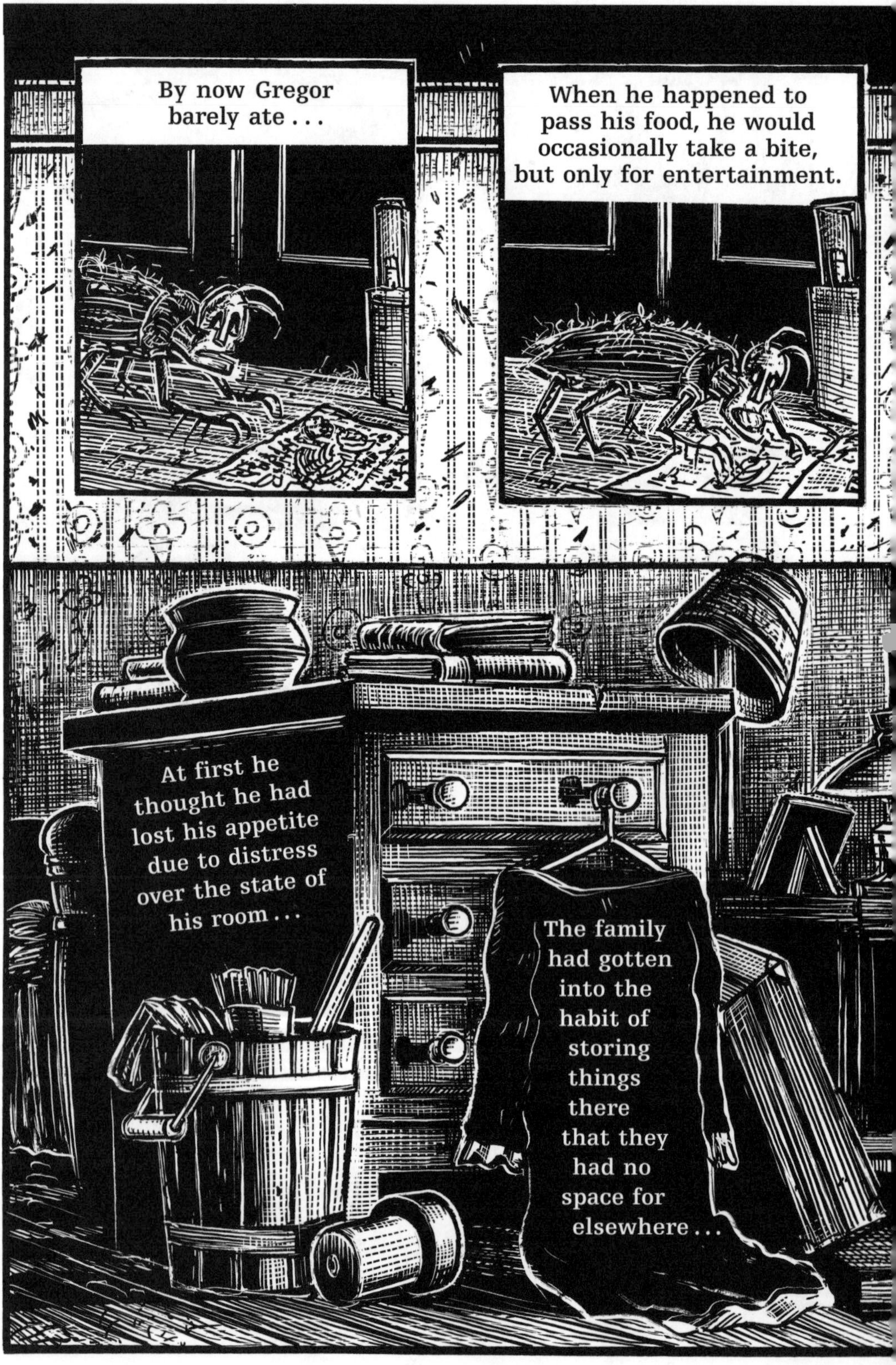
By now Gregor barely ate . . .
When he happened to pass his food, he would occasionally take a bite, but only for entertainment.
At first he thought he had lost his appetite due to distress over the state of his room . . .
The family had gotten into the habit of storing things there that they had no space for elsewhere . . .

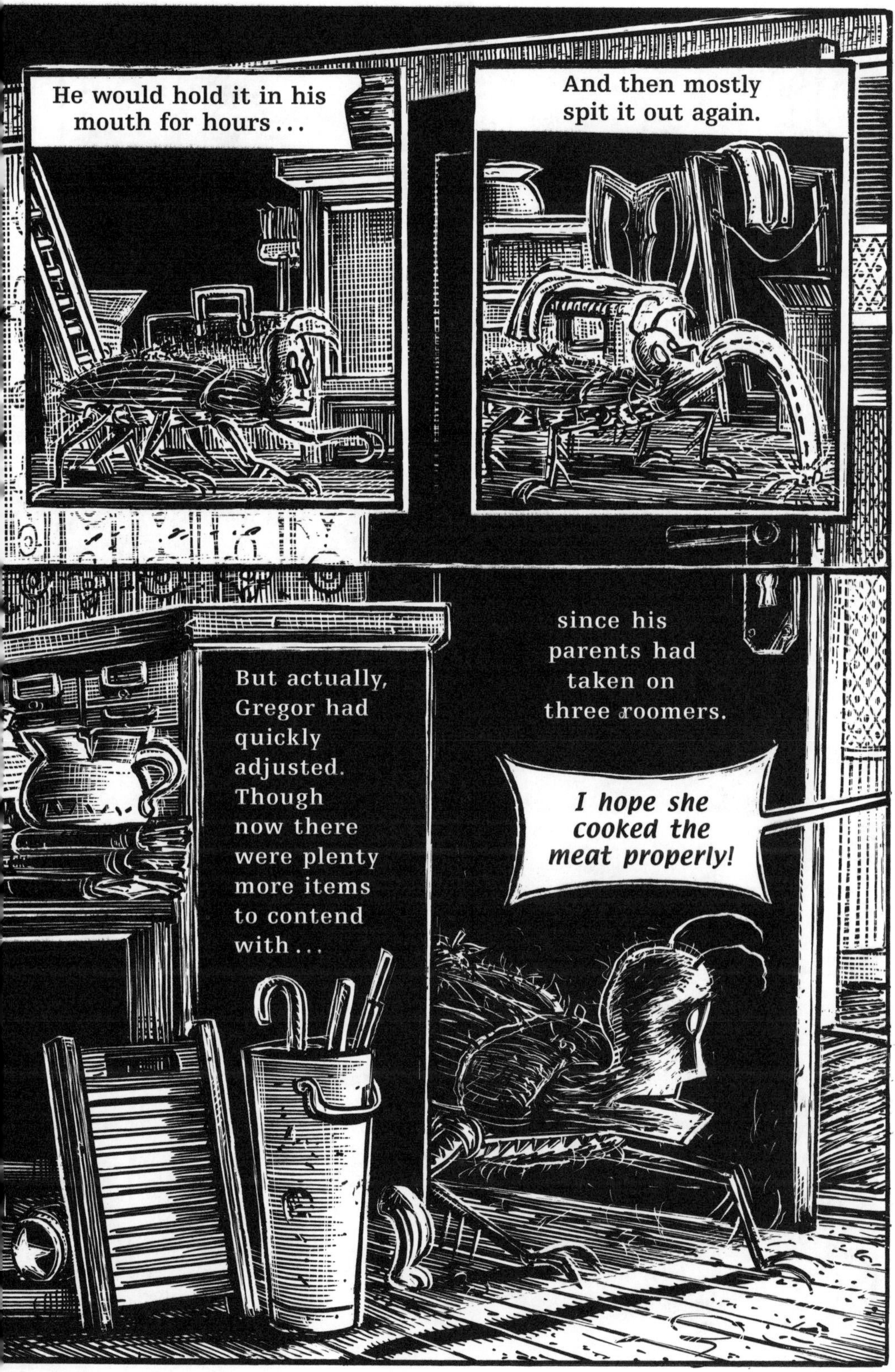
He would hold it in his mouth for hours...
And then mostly spit it out again.
But actually, Gregor had quickly adjusted. Though now there were plenty more items to contend with...
since his parents had taken on three roomers.
I hope she cooked the meat properly!

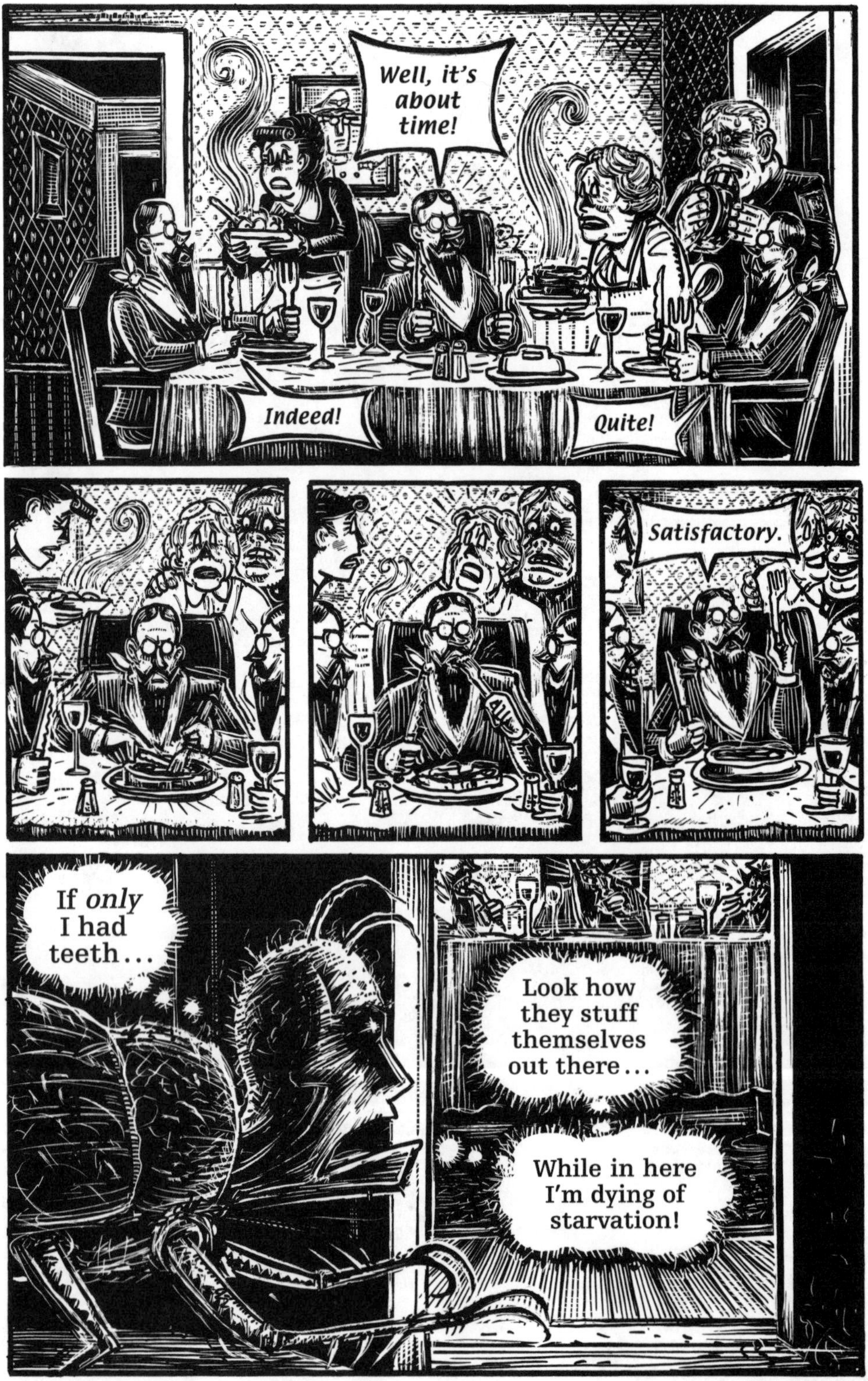
Well, it's about time!
Indeed!
Quite!
Satisfactory.
If *only* I had teeth...
Look how they stuff themselves out there...
While in here I'm dying of starvation!

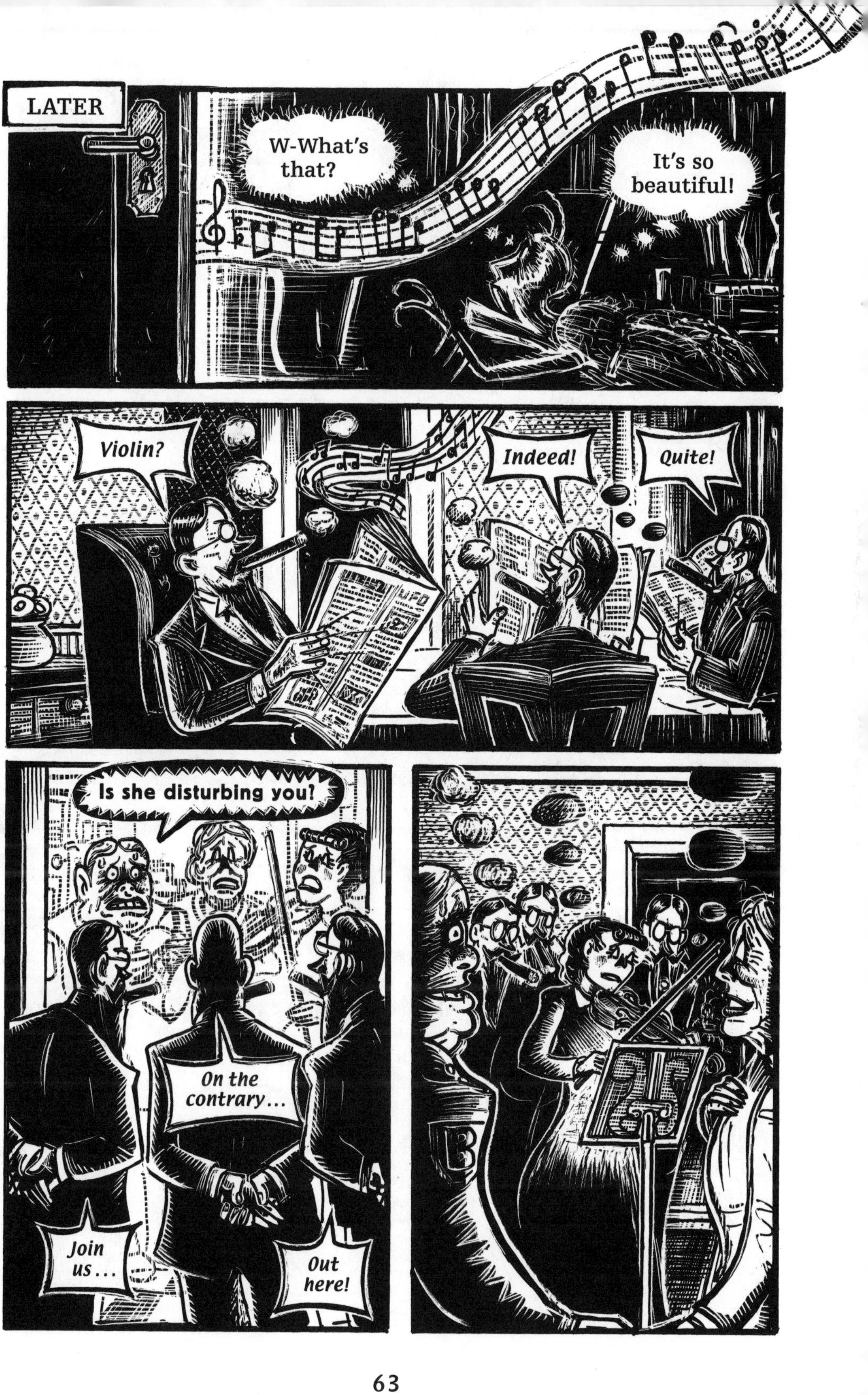
LATER
W-What's that?
It's so beautiful!
Violin?
Indeed!
Quite!
Is she disturbing you?
On the contrary...
Join us...
Out here!

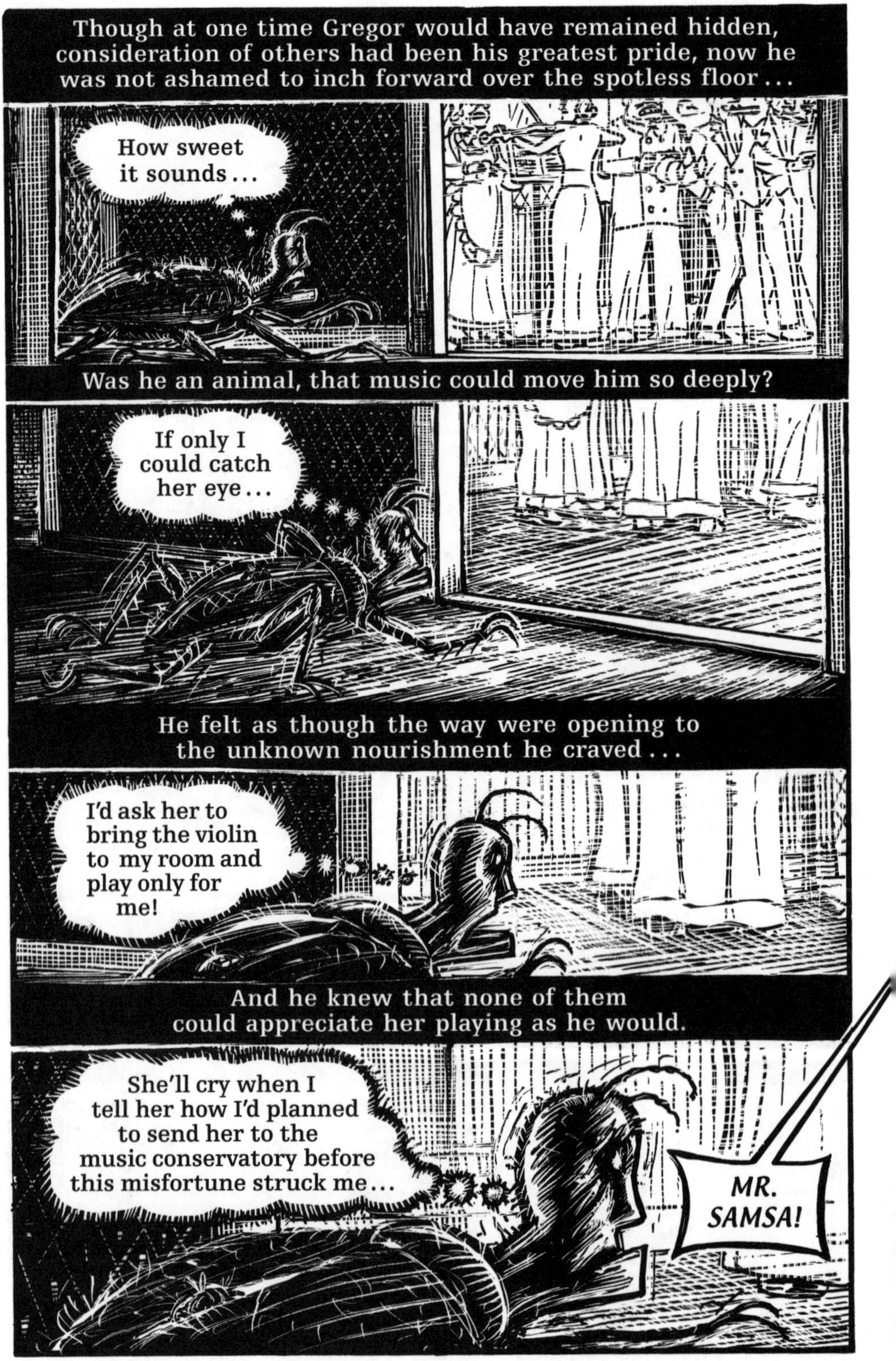

Though at one time Gregor would have remained hidden, consideration of others had been his greatest pride, now he was not ashamed to inch forward over the spotless floor . . .
How sweet it sounds . . .
Was he an animal, that music could move him so deeply?
If only I could catch her eye . . .
He felt as though the way were opening to the unknown nourishment he craved . . .
I'd ask her to bring the violin to my room and play only for me!
And he knew that none of them could appreciate her playing as he would.
She'll cry when I tell her how I'd planned to send her to the music conservatory before this misfortune struck me . . .
MR. SAMSA!

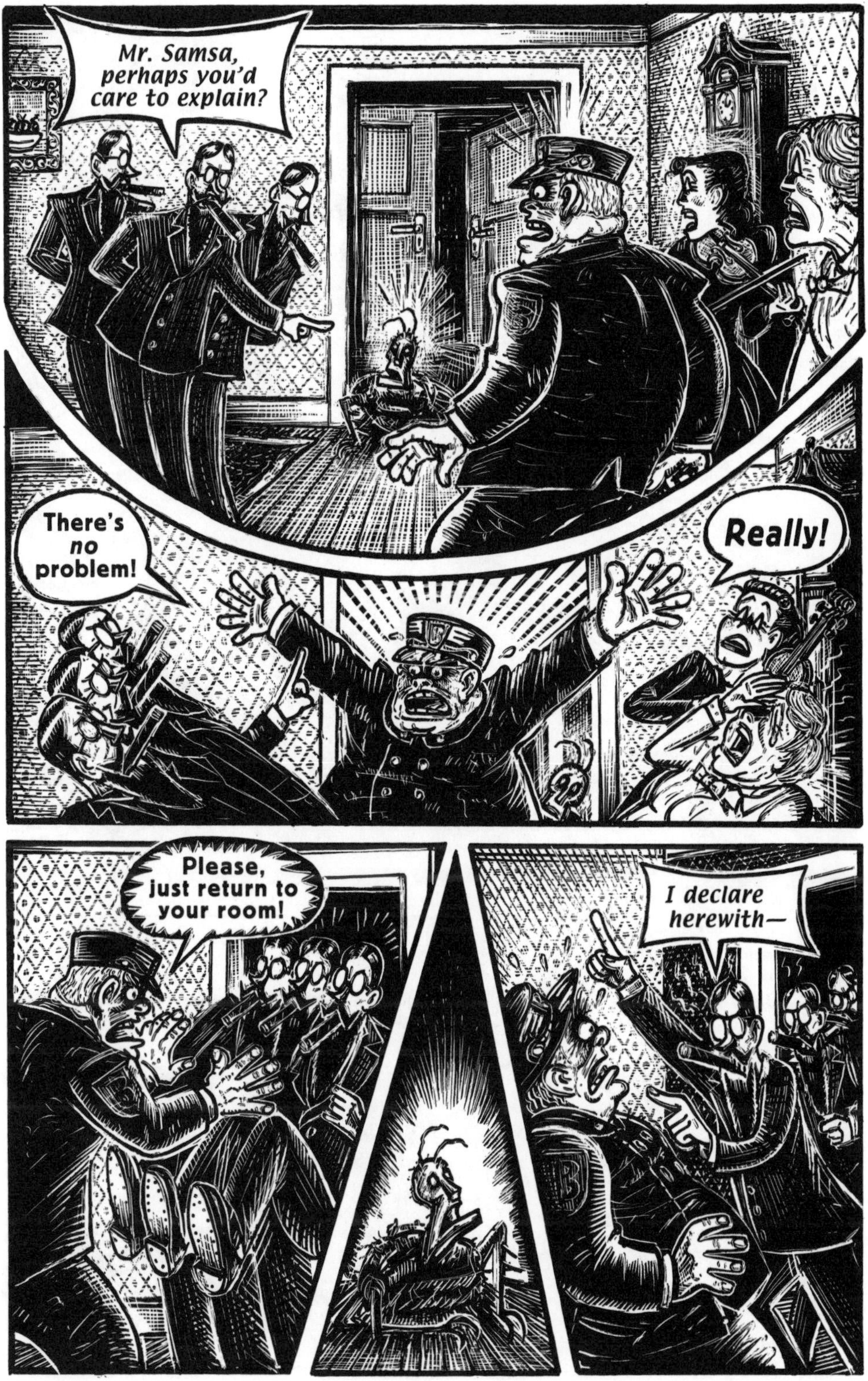
Mr. Samsa, perhaps you'd care to explain?
There's *no* problem!
Really!
Please, just return to your room!
I declare herewith—

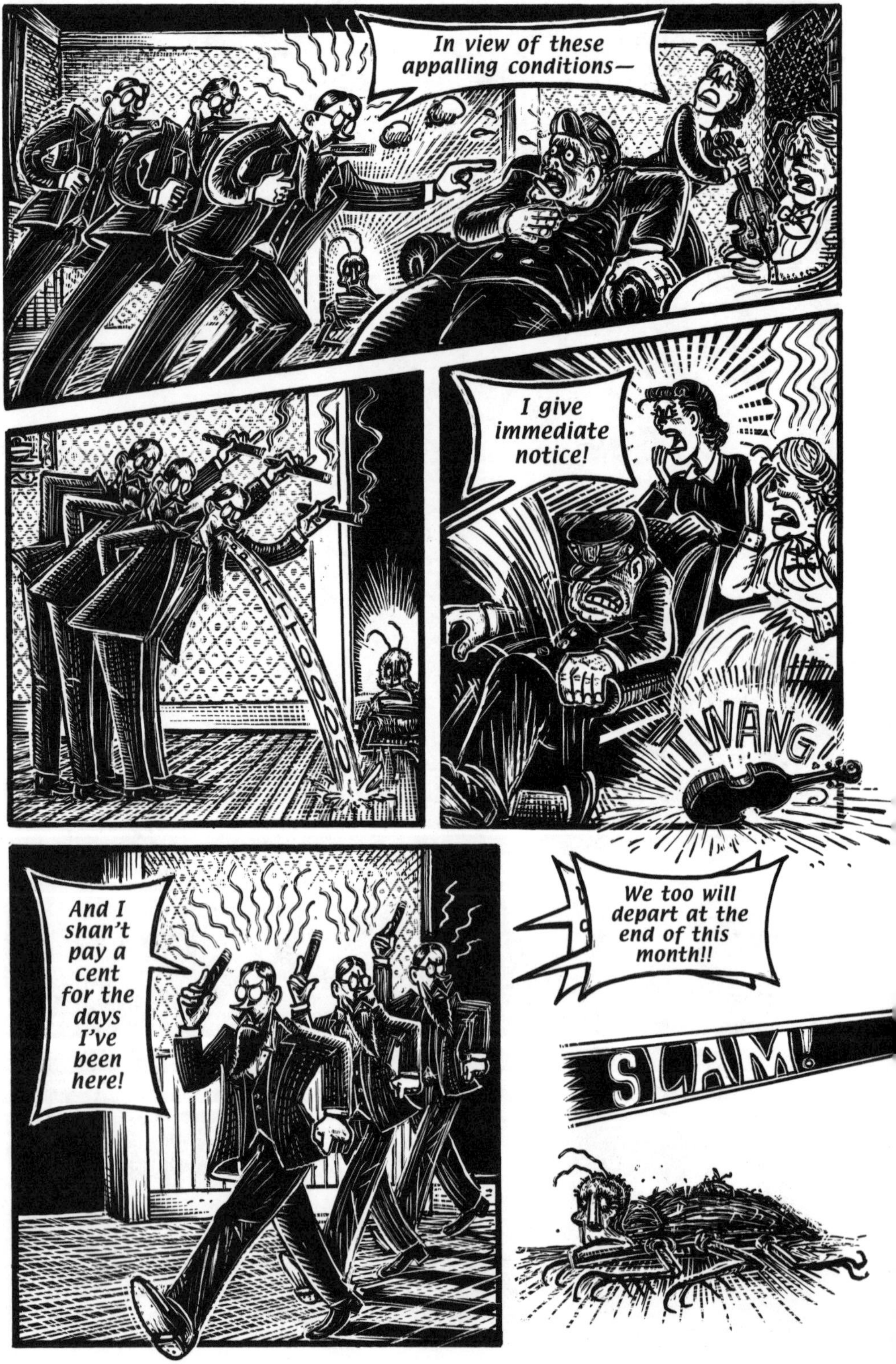
In view of these appalling conditions—
I give immediate notice!
TWANG!
And I shan't pay a cent for the days I've been here!
We too will depart at the end of this month!!
SLAM!

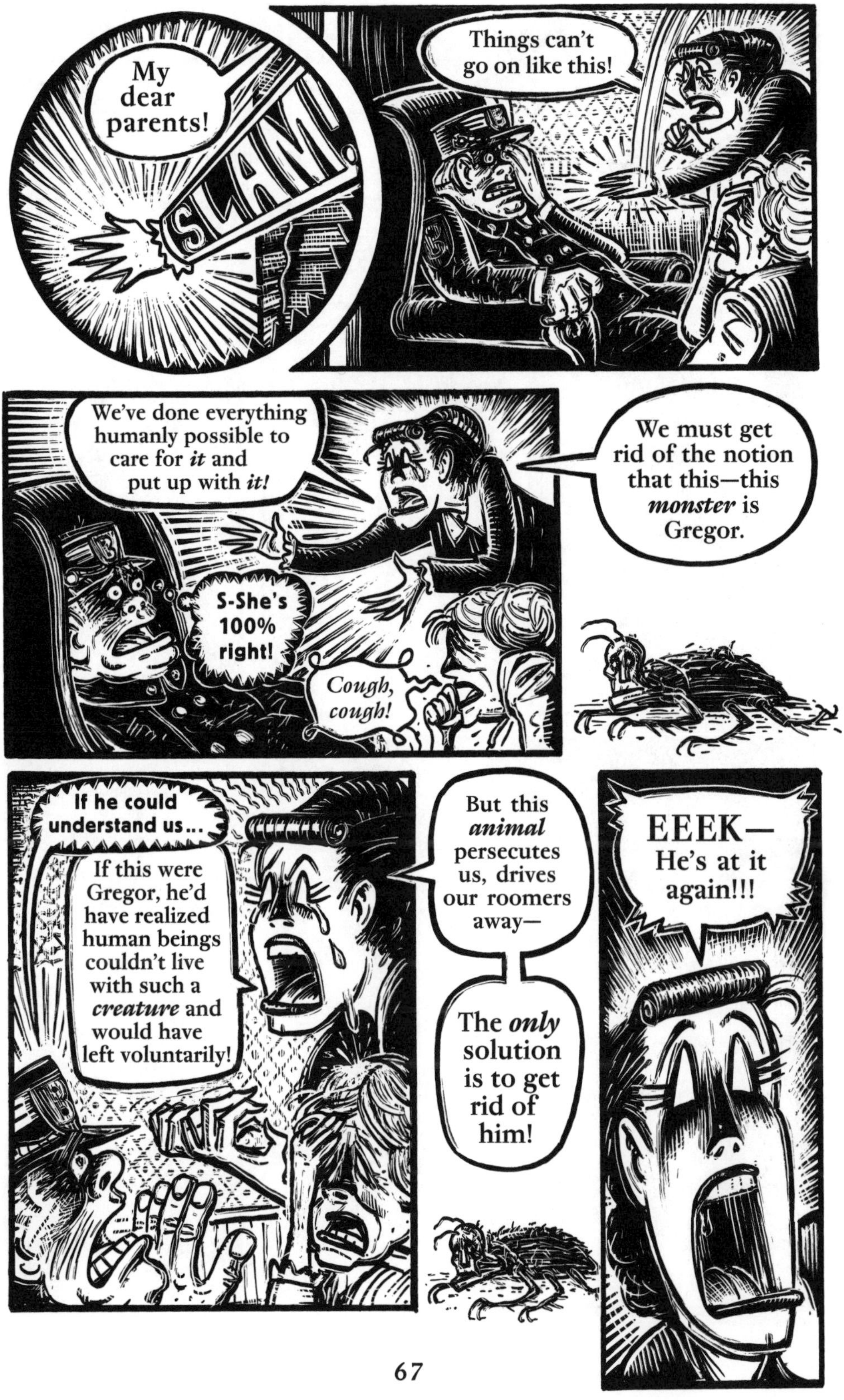
My dear parents!
SLAM!
Things can't go on like this!
We've done everything humanly possible to care for *it* and put up with *it!*
We must get rid of the notion that this—this *monster* is Gregor.
S-She's 100% right!
Cough, cough!
If he could understand us...
If this were Gregor, he'd have realized human beings couldn't live with such a *creature* and would have left voluntarily!
But this *animal* persecutes us, drives our roomers away—
The *only* solution is to get rid of him!
EEEK— He's at it again!!!

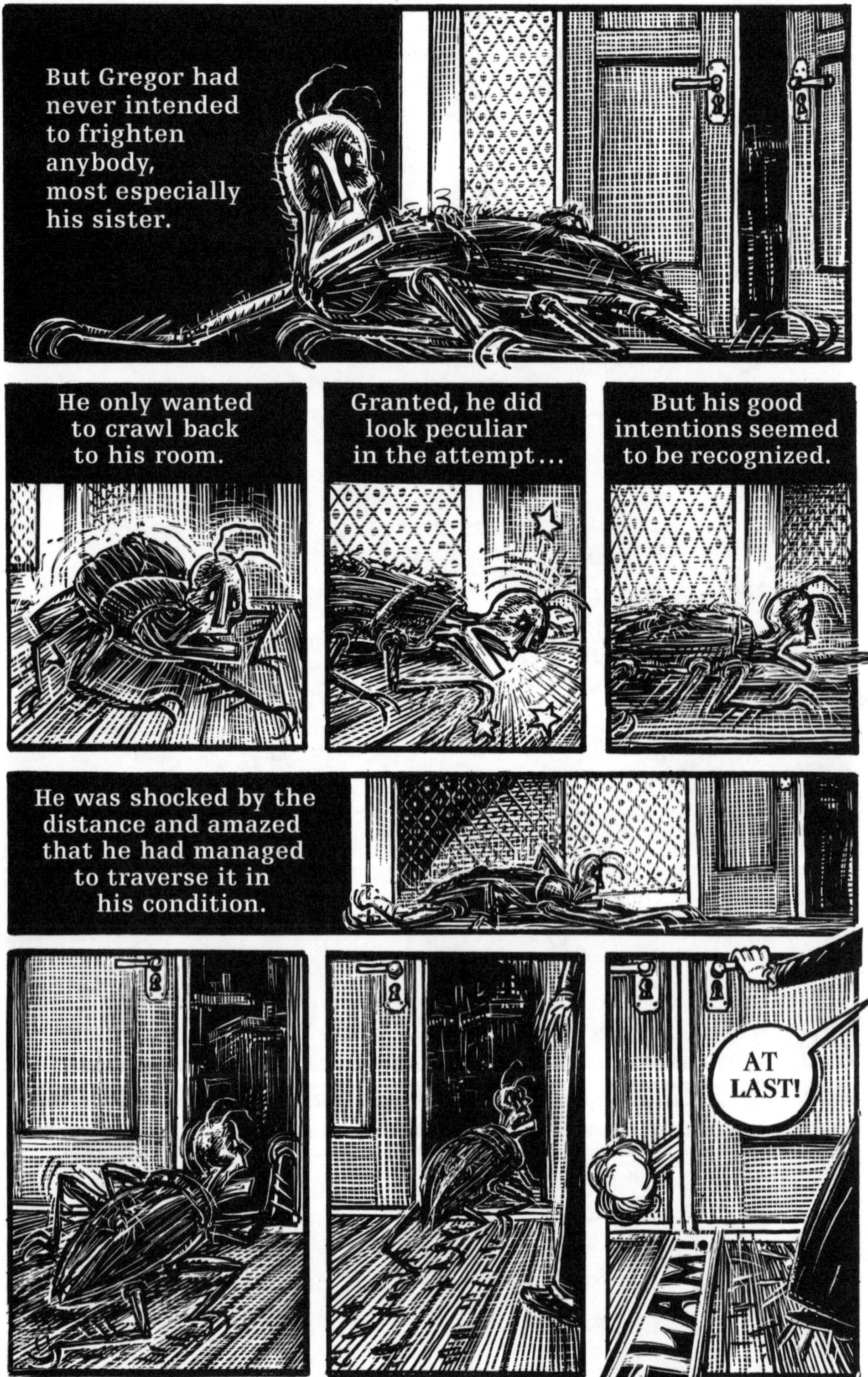
But Gregor had never intended to frighten anybody, most especially his sister.
He only wanted to crawl back to his room.
Granted, he did look peculiar in the attempt...
But his good intentions seemed to be recognized.
He was shocked by the distance and amazed that he had managed to traverse it in his condition.
AT LAST!
SLAM!

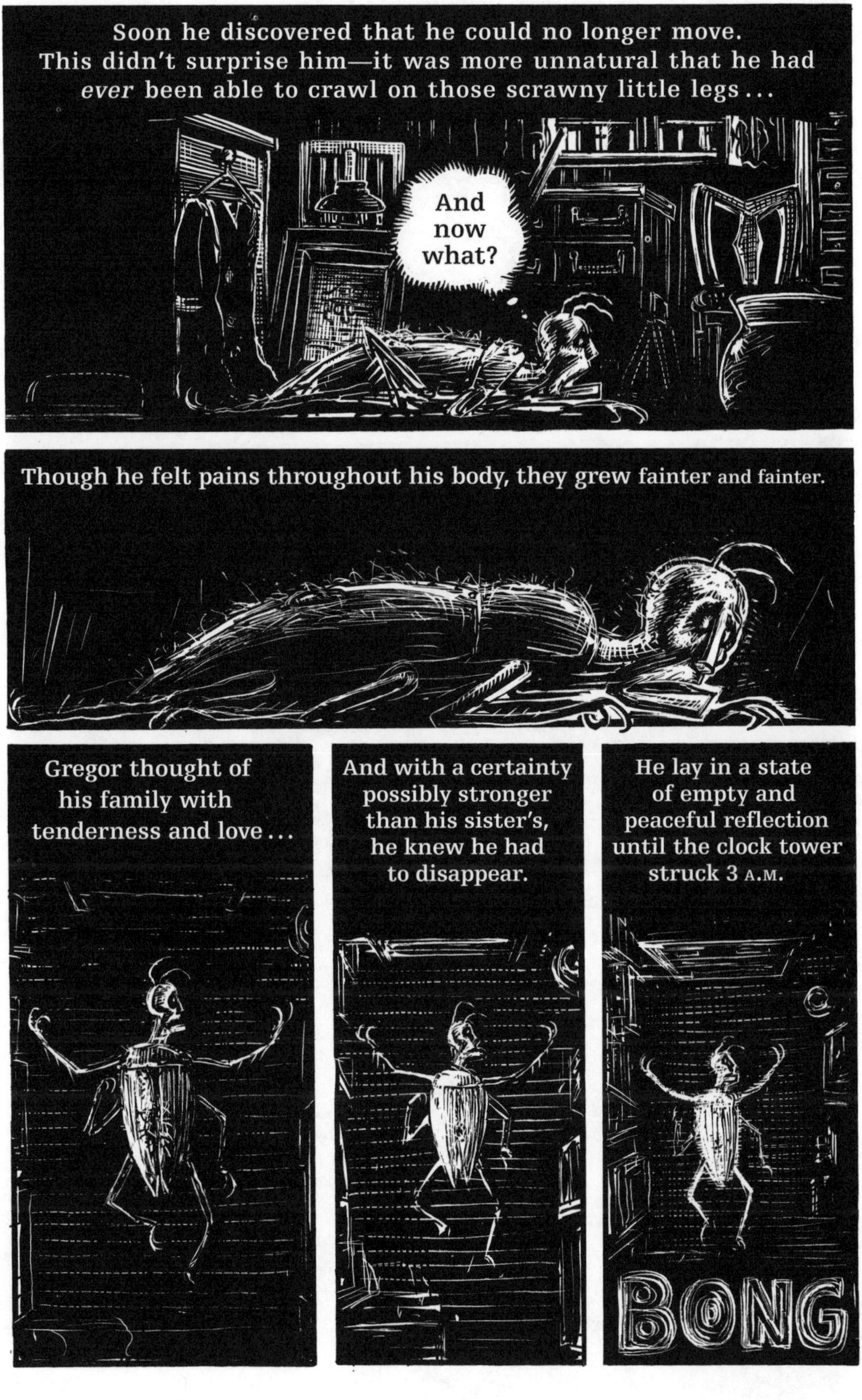
Soon he discovered that he could no longer move. This didn't surprise him—it was more unnatural that he had *ever* been able to crawl on those scrawny little legs...
And now what?
Though he felt pains throughout his body, they grew fainter and fainter.
Gregor thought of his family with tenderness and love...
And with a certainty possibly stronger than his sister's, he knew he had to disappear.
He lay in a state of empty and peaceful reflection until the clock tower struck 3 A.M.
BONG

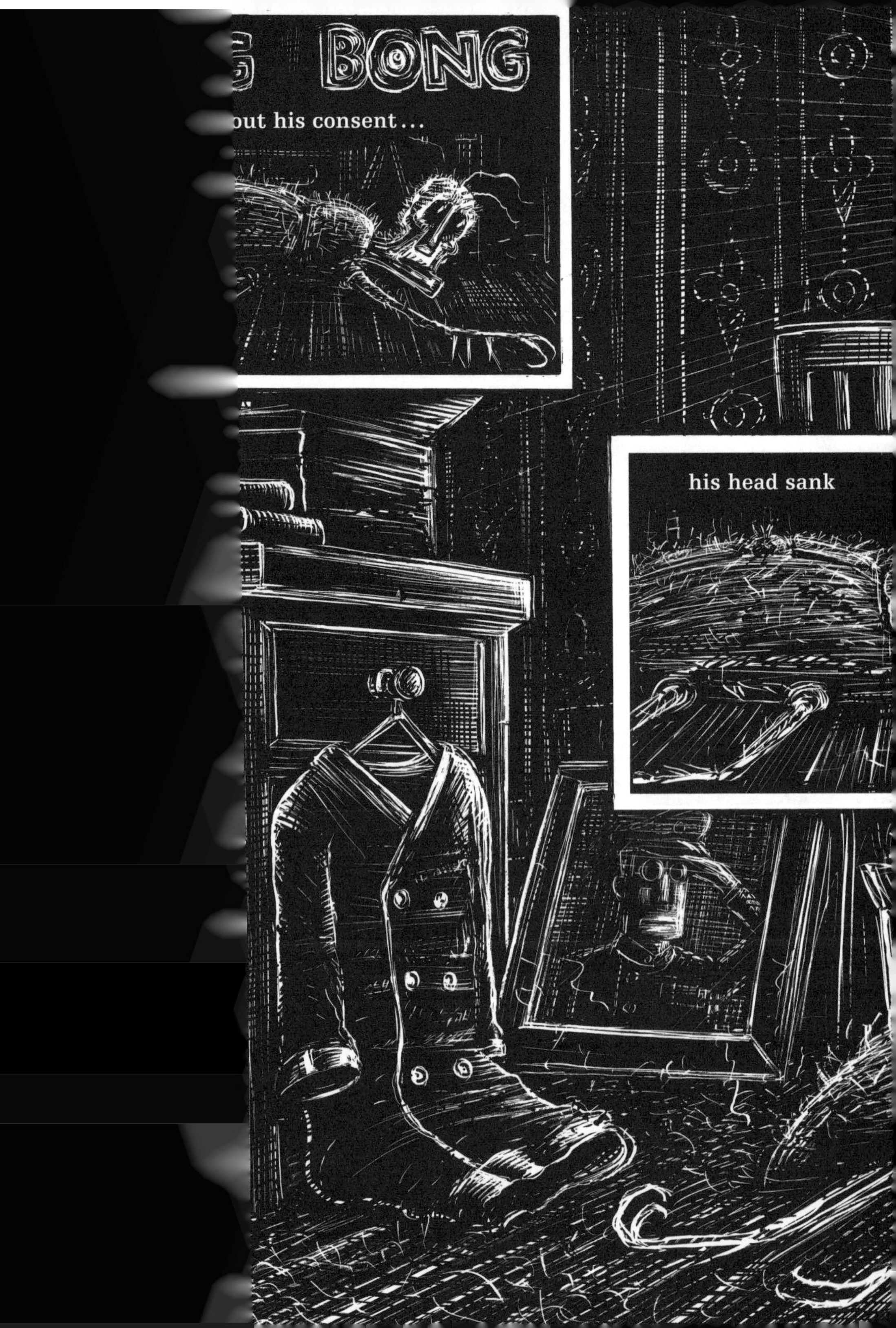

G BONG
out his consent...
his head sank

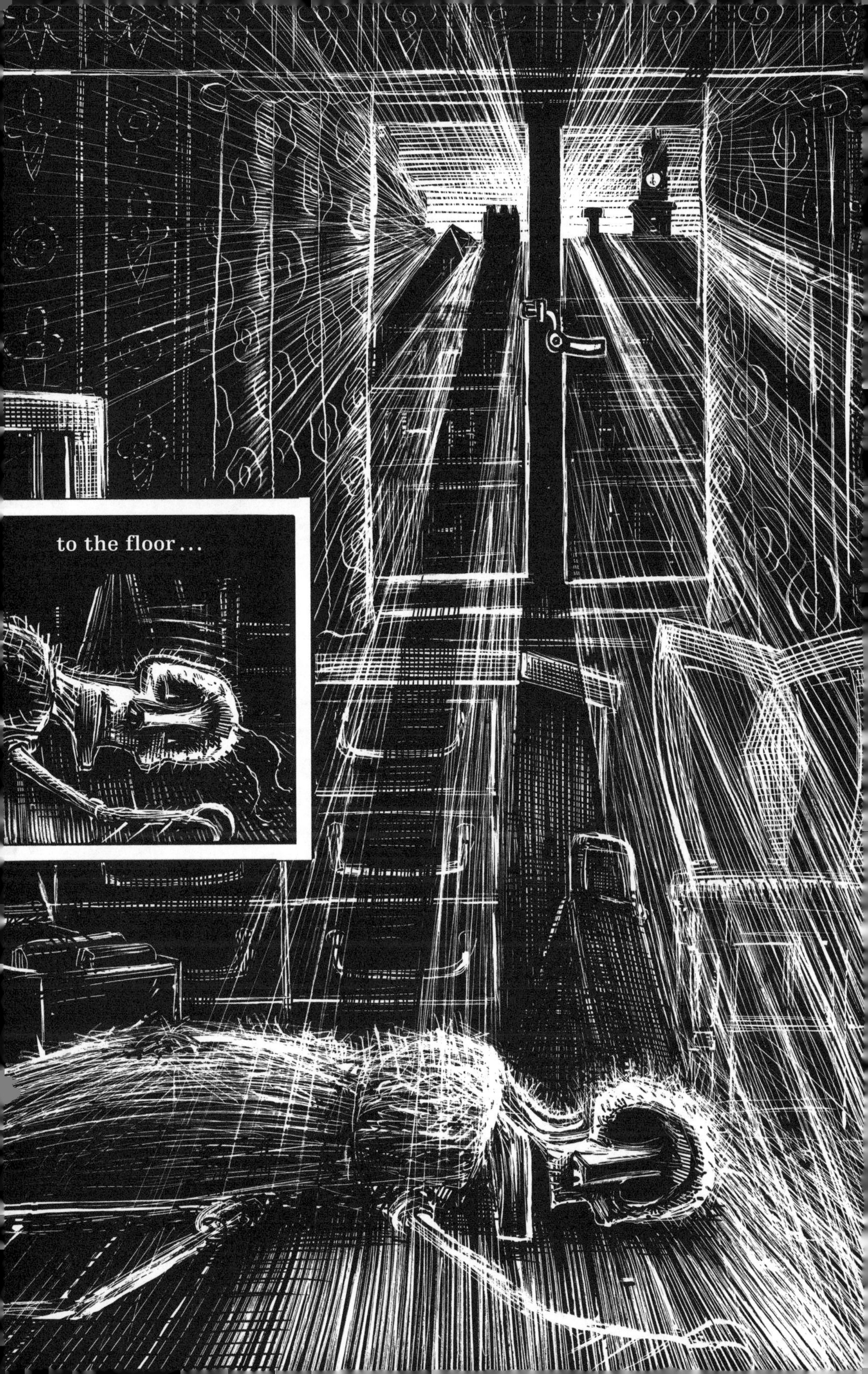
to the floor...

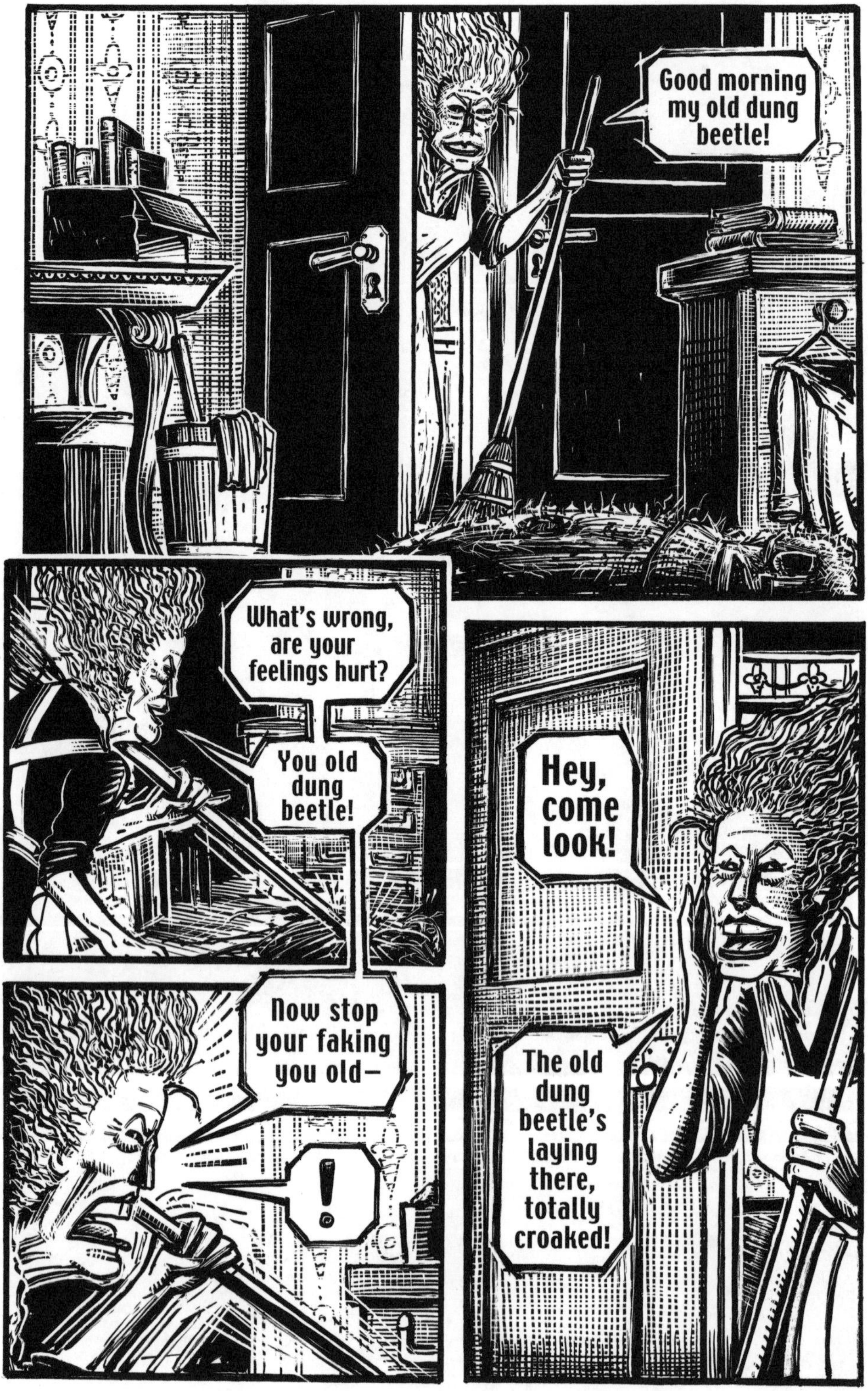
Good morning my old dung beetle!
What's wrong, are your feelings hurt?
You old dung beetle!
Now stop your faking you old–
!
Hey, come look!
The old dung beetle's laying there, totally croaked!

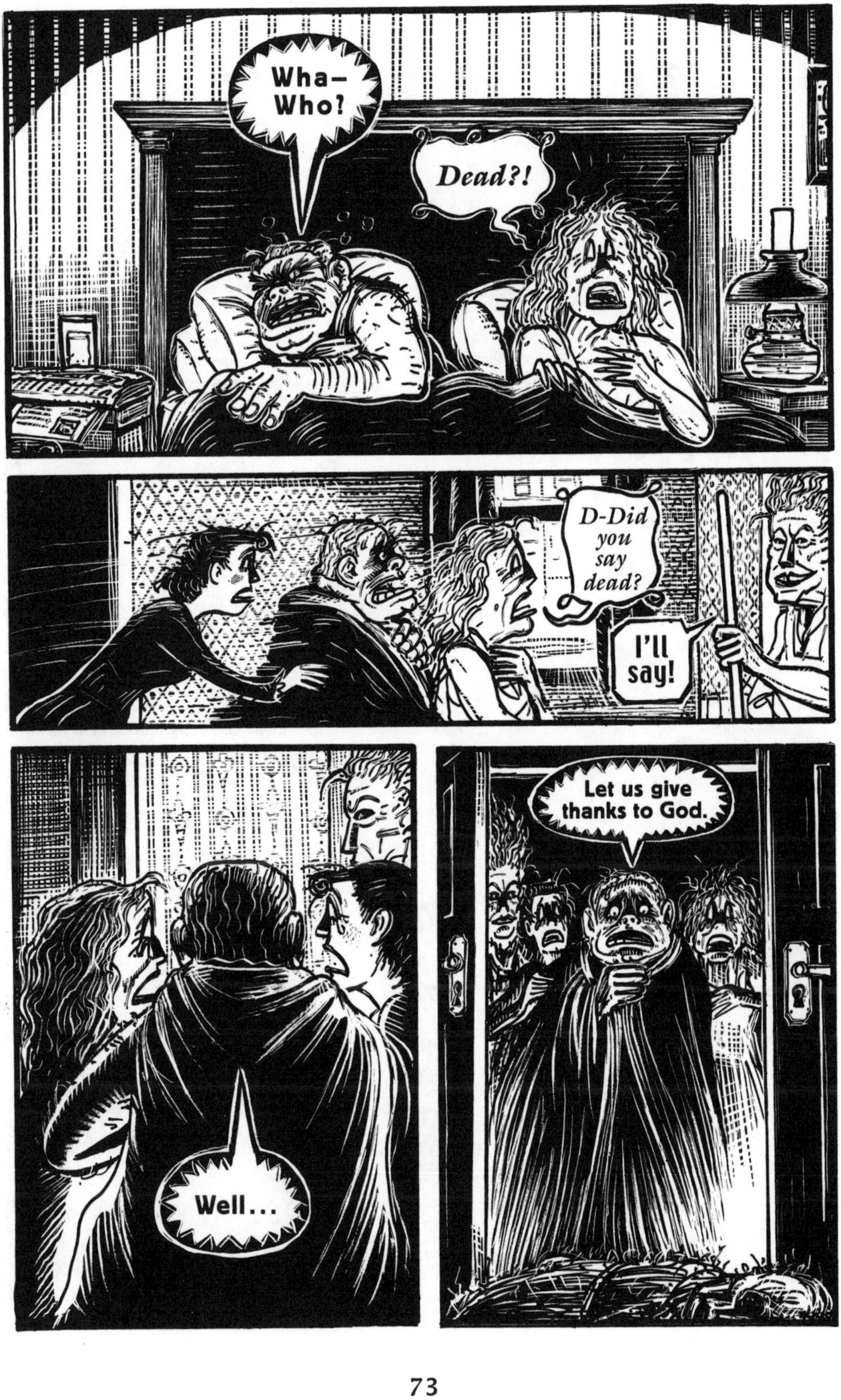
Wha–
Who?
Dead?!
D-Did you say dead?
I'll say!
Well...
Let us give thanks to God.

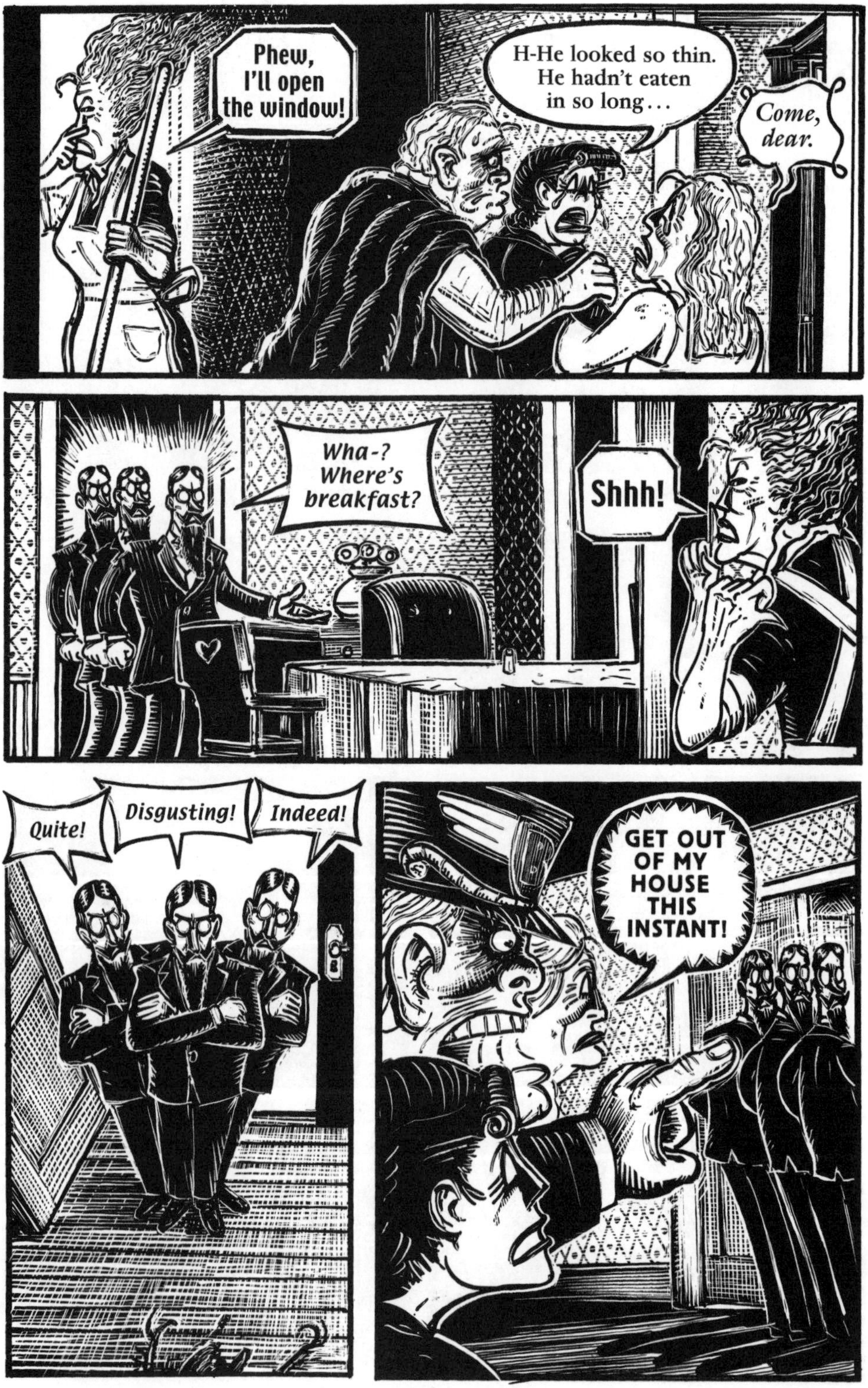
Phew, I'll open the window!
H-He looked so thin. He hadn't eaten in so long...
Come, dear.
Wha-? Where's breakfast?
Shhh!
Quite!
Disgusting!
Indeed!
GET OUT OF MY HOUSE THIS INSTANT!

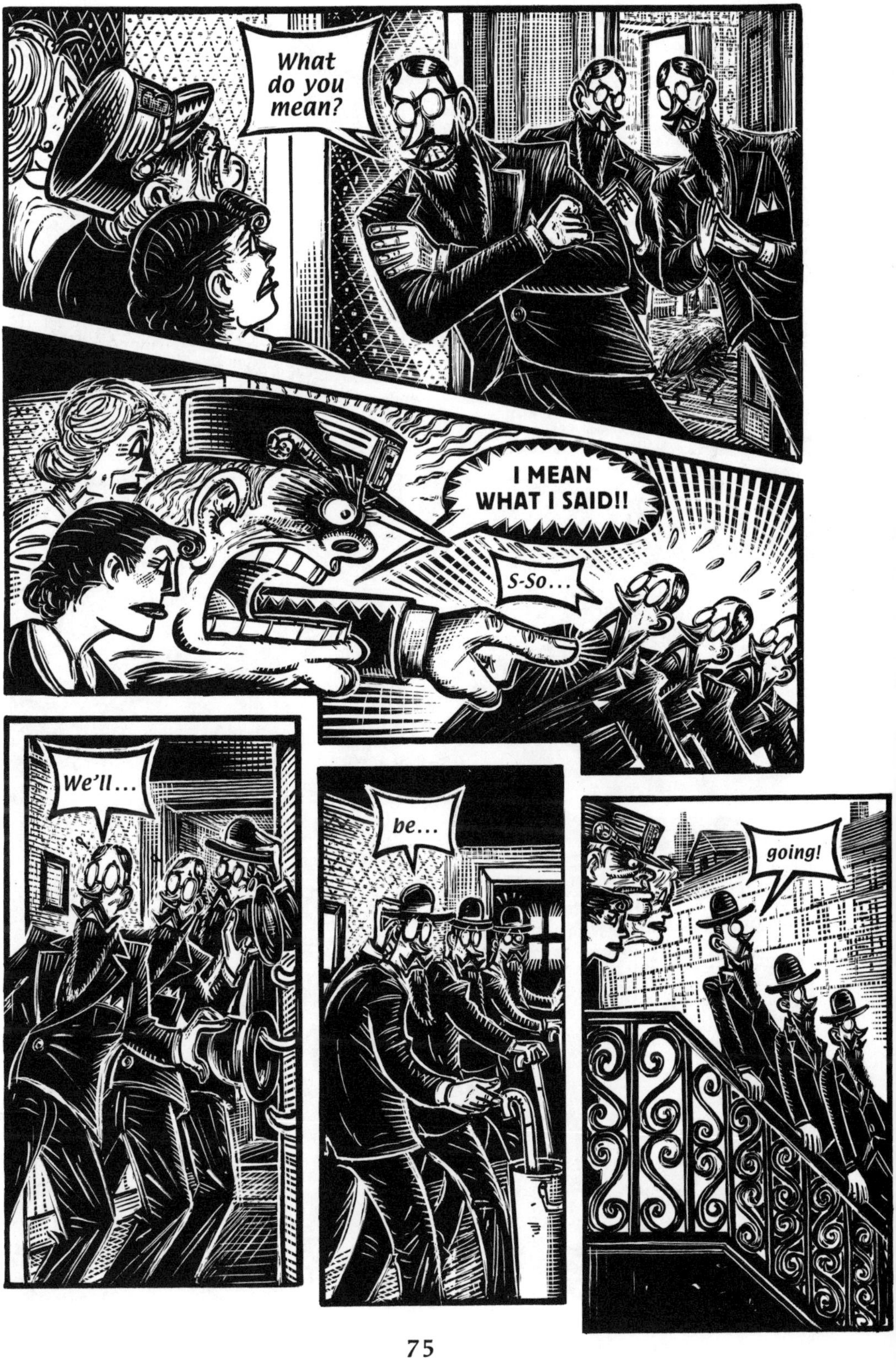
What do you mean?
I MEAN WHAT I SAID!!
S-So...
We'll...
be...
going!

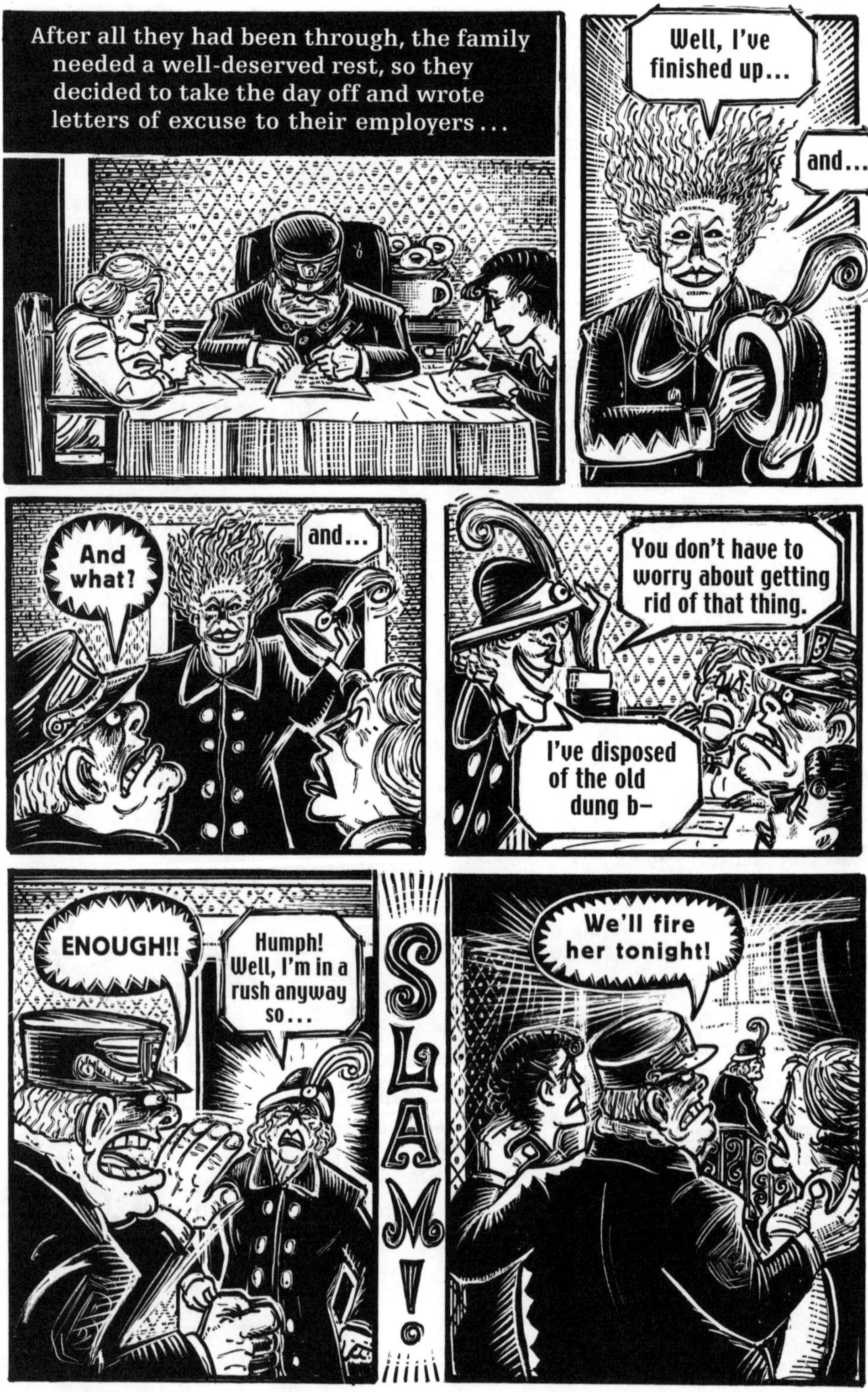

After all they had been through, the family needed a well-deserved rest, so they decided to take the day off and wrote letters of excuse to their employers...
Well, I've finished up...
and...
And what?
and...
You don't have to worry about getting rid of that thing.
I've disposed of the old dung b–
ENOUGH!!
Humph! Well, I'm in a rush anyway so...
SLAM!
We'll fire her tonight!

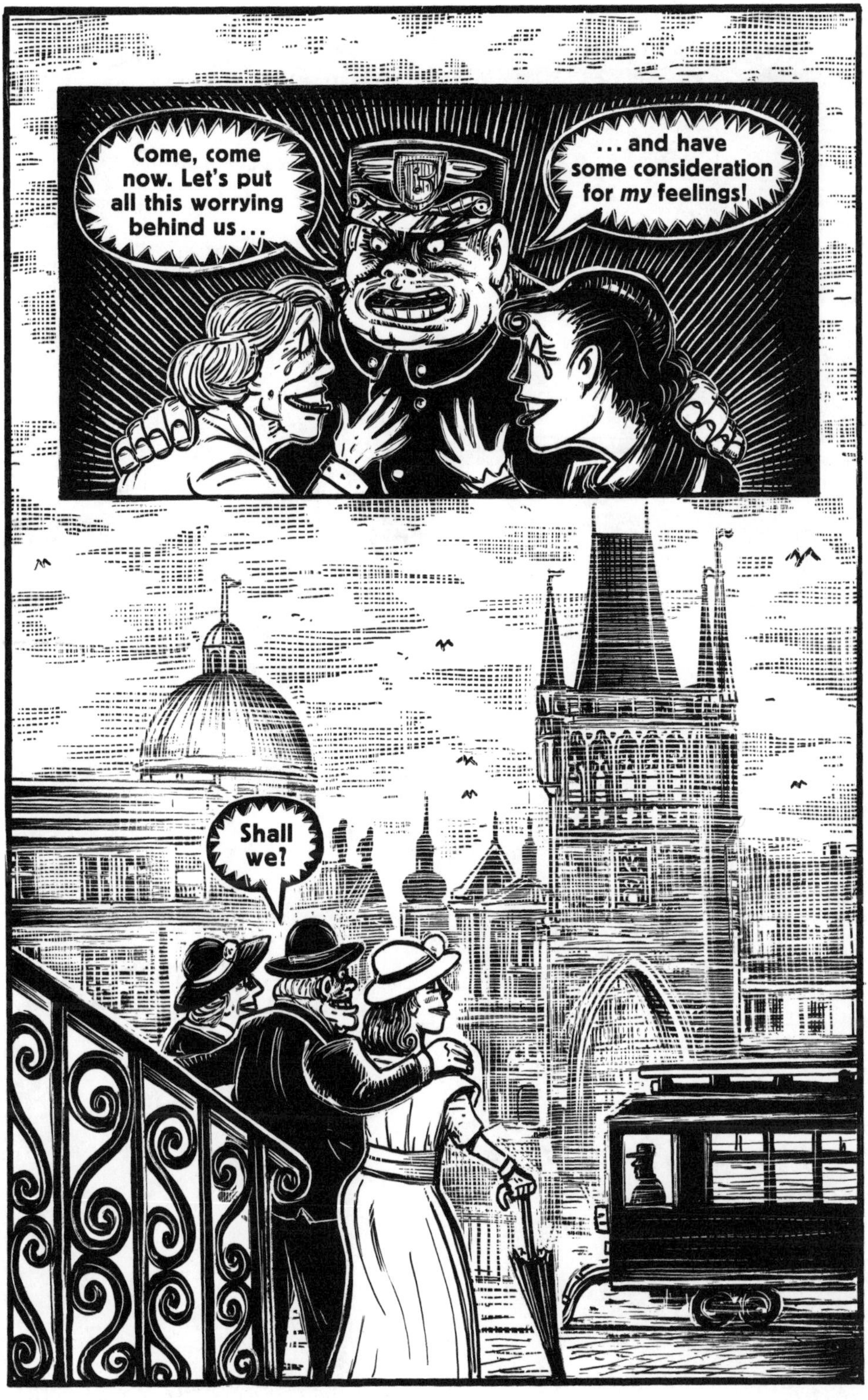
Come, come now. Let's put all this worrying behind us...
...and have some consideration for *my* feelings!
Shall we?

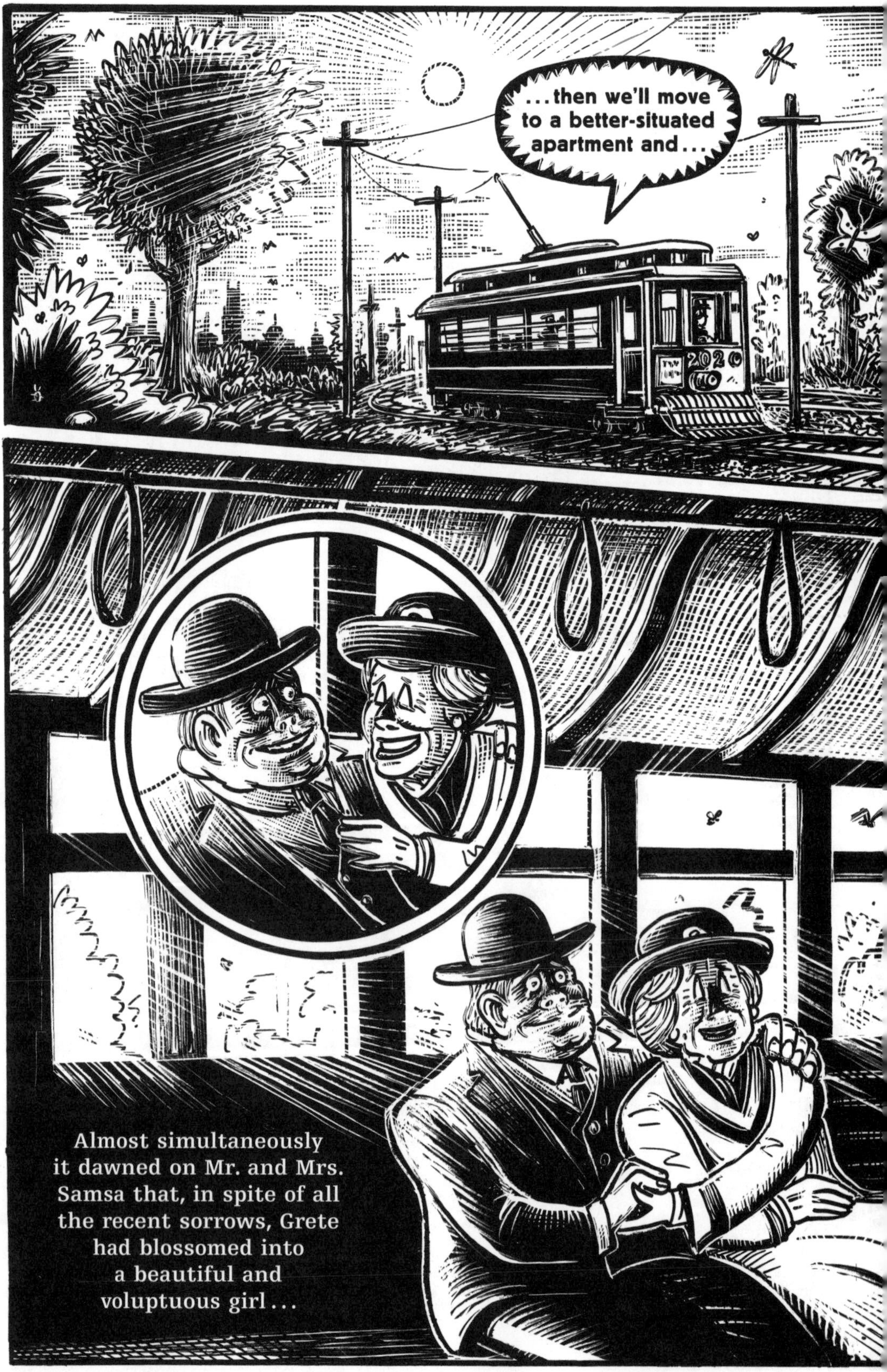
...then we'll move to a better-situated apartment and...
2020
Almost simultaneously it dawned on Mr. and Mrs. Samsa that, in spite of all the recent sorrows, Grete had blossomed into a beautiful and voluptuous girl...

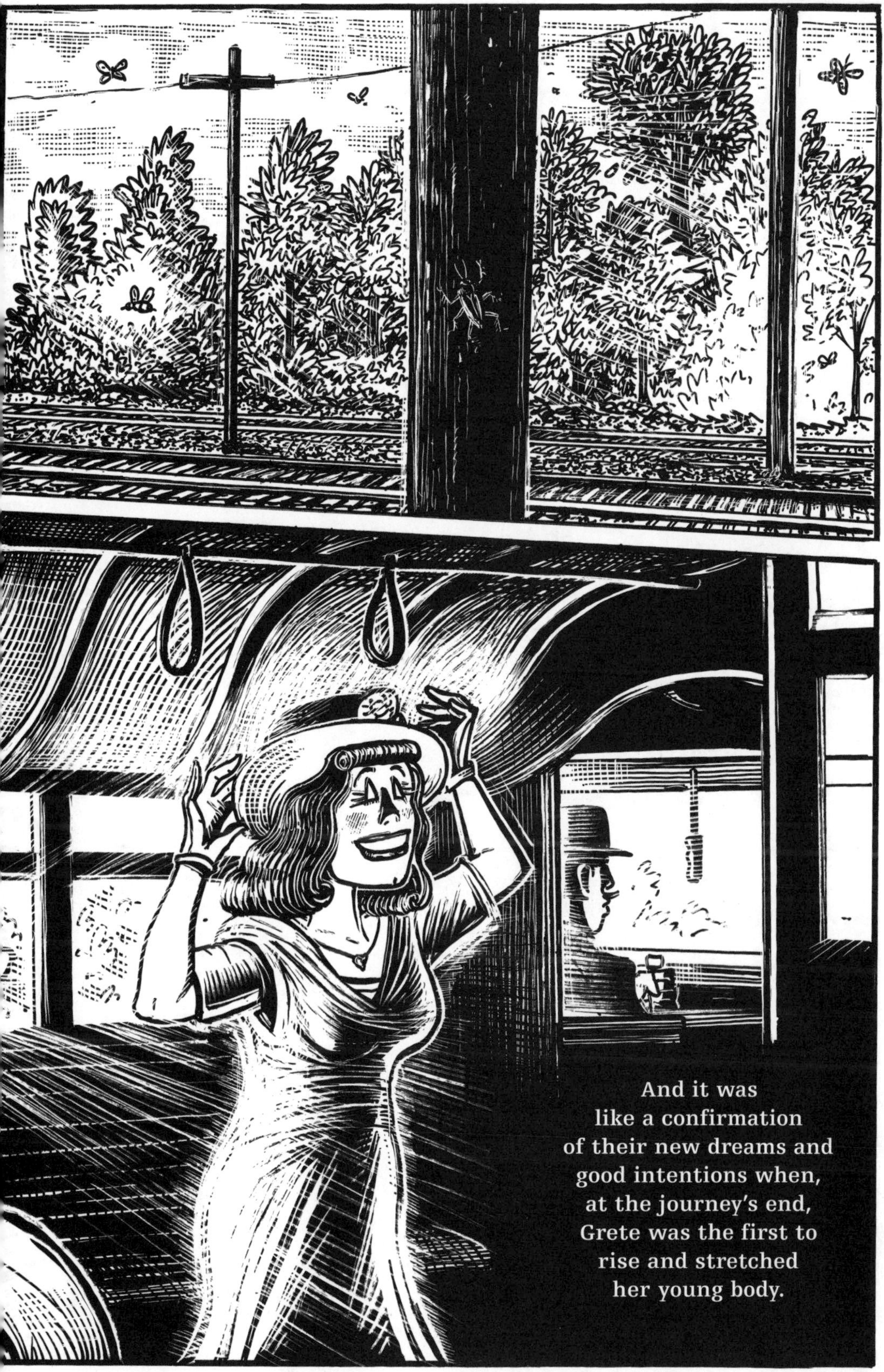
And it was like a confirmation of their new dreams and good intentions when, at the journey's end, Grete was the first to rise and stretched her young body.

ABOUT THE ARTIST

PETER KUPER was born in 1958 and grew up in Cleveland, Ohio. He moved to New York City in 1977 and attended Pratt Institute in Brooklyn. Peter is cofounder of the political magazine *World War 3 Illustrated,* which he has coedited over the last 23 years, and has taught courses in comics at the School of Visual Arts since 1986. He has written and illustrated numerous graphic novels, including *Give It Up!,* his first collection of Franz Kafka adaptations, *The System, Eye of the Beholder, Stripped,* and *Comics Trips,* which chronicles an eight-month trip through Africa and Southeast Asia. His previous book, *Speechless,* is a career retrospective.

Peter's illustrations appear regularly in many magazines and newspapers, including *Time,* the *New York Times,* and *MAD,* for which he draws *Spy Vs. Spy* every month. His work can be seen on the Web at www.peterkuper.com.

ACKNOWLEDGMENTS

Thanks and appreciation to a great number of people
who helped bring this project to light:

my beautiful wife, Betty Russell,
for all her marvelous suggestions and eternal patience;

Steve Ross, my longtime friend,
and Chris Jackson, my diligent editor, at Crown;

Terry Nantier at NBM for years of support;

Ryan Inzana for his endless assistance;

John Thomas for lending his legal expertise;

Emily Russell for her fantastic editorial eye;

Kerstin Hasenpusch for a fine job of translating;

Susy Bernstein for her scholarly perspective;

Gahan Wilson, Will Eisner, and Jules Feiffer
for their ongoing encouragement;

my ever supportive family;

my friends Tony, Molly, Philip, Scott, Elena, and Seth;

and especially my daughter, Emily, for "bug book" enthusiasms.

Finally, thanks to Franz Kafka, who was kind enough to put
pen to paper in the first place and create a masterpiece.

10/03

BAKER & TAYLOR